Marlow— a great actor on the stage, a man of many masks in his crowded private life

Cynthia— his mistress, victim of his charm and slave of his desires

David— his illegitimate son, growing up to be his rival and fighting not to be his puppet

Barbara—a wanton beauty who hungered for love from the man to whom she had given too much too soon

These are the players. The stage is set for Death. And Toby Marlow begins the most difficult and exalted role of a long and brilliant career. He has always lived in high style, and why should his *exit* be any less flamboyant?

THE MARLOW
CHRONICLES

LAWRENCE SANDERS

The Marlow Chronicles

BERKLEY BOOKS, NEW YORK

This Berkley book contains the complete
text of the original hardcover edition.
It has been completely reset in a type face
designed for easy reading, and was printed
from new film.

THE MARLOW CHRONICLES

A Berkley Book / published by arrangement with
G. P. Putnam's Sons

PRINTING HISTORY
G. P. Putnam's Sons edition published April 1977
Berkley edition / December 1979
3 printings through 1980

ISBN: 0-425-04390-8

A BERKLEY BOOK ® TM 757,375
Berkley Books are published by Berkley Publishing Corporation,
200 Madison Avenue, New York, New York 10016.
PRINTED IN THE UNITED STATES OF AMERICA

The Marlow Chronicles

ACT ONE

SCENE ONE

HE SAT ON THE EDGE of the receptionist's desk, leaned over, peered down her neckline.

"I once knew a mountain range that looked like you," he said. "The Grand Tetons."

"Oh Mr. Marlow!" She giggled.

"Are you really a widow, Suzy?" he asked.

"Twice," she said. "Both my husbands are deceased."

"What from—exhaustion?"

He swung off the desk, tried to straighten up, clasped a hand to his ribs.

"Are you all right?" she asked anxiously. "Maybe you should be home in bed."

"Splendid idea," he said. "Let's go."

He stalked around the office, trying to draw deep breaths. It hurt.

"I was sorry to hear you were in the hospital, Mr. Marlow," she said. "I hope it wasn't anything serious."

"I was being examined for the Guinness Book of World Records," he said. "They just wouldn't believe. Where *is* that man?"

"He should be here any minute. He knew you were coming today."

"Then he's one up on my wife. I'm going into his office and make a phone call."

"Mr. Ostretter doesn't like the phone being used for personal calls."

"I know, Suzy," Toby Marlow said. "He's so mean he farts in elevators. I'll leave you a dime on the way out."

He went into Julius Ostretter's private office, sat in his swivel chair, put his feet up on the polished desk. He called Hollywood, then held his ribs with one hand. The phone was answered on the third ring.

"Hi ya, baby," Marlow said, "I love you, too.... Who is this?... Who?... The *bookie?* Leo's got a bookie who makes house calls? Now I know where his ten percent goes. Put him on, will you?... Leo? Hiya, baby... I love you, too... Leo, what's with Universal?... Who got the job?... You gotta be kidding! Isn't he the guy with a gold ring in his nose?... I know, Leo, but for *Martin Luther?*... Okay, forget it. Who's playing Queen Elizabeth?... Listen, Leo, Harry just hasn't got the panache.... I know he does that, but I said *panache.* It's French for chutzpah.... Oh? He does that, too?"

Julius Ostretter came striding into the office, carrying a black attaché case. He glared angrily at the man behind his desk.

"Okay, Leo, I've got to run; I'm double-parked. Tell

everyone out there I'm in perfect health and ready to get back to work.... Right.... Will do.... Love you too, baby."

He hung up and glared back at Ostretter.

"Where were you calling?" the lawyer demanded.

"Hong Kong," Marlow said. "Where the hell have you been?"

"So I'm a little late," Ostretter said. "I was watching the Hungarians parade."

"How much did they charge?" Toby Marlow asked.

"So what's so important it can't wait a few minutes? Get out of my chair."

"Julius, for God's sake, I'm practically an invalid, and you'd make me move?"

Grumbling, Ostretter took the leather club chair alongside the desk.

"All right," he said, "so what's the emergency?"

"I got a nasty letter from the government."

"Where is it?"

"In Washington, D.C."

"Come on, Toby, the letter...where is the letter?"

"I tore it up and flushed it down the kazoo. From the IRS, the bastards. They claim I owe more taxes. Julius, what does the government *do* with all my money?"

"The FBI..."

"I got mugged twice this year."

"The armed forces..."

"Last night a sailor propositioned me."

"Aid to underdeveloped nations..."

"Hah! Last week the ambassador from Nigeria got *my* table at the Chantilly. I tell you, Julius, the government lives in luxury and I live in squalor."

"Last year you tried to deduct fifty percent of your rent as a business expense."

"Fifty percent! That doesn't even pay for my vodka."

"I told you it wouldn't work. How are you feeling?"

"Lousy. Your brother is coming over this afternoon to—"

"Stop!" Ostretter shouted, holding up a hand. "Don't mention that creature's name! I don't want to hear a word about him!"

"All right, already. Calm down. I swear I won't mention the name of Jacob Ostretter."

Julius Ostretter groaned.

"So what should I do? About the letter?"

"Pay them what you owe, Toby. So the government can buy another destroyer."

"A destroyer I wouldn't mind. But the Sixth Fleet? Ah, screw it. I'll fight it. Let them take me to court."

"You'll lose," Julius Ostretter said.

"Then I'll appeal and appeal and appeal. I'll take it to the highest court!"

"That'll be some vote," the lawyer said. "Nine to nothing."

"Not the Supreme Court, dummy," Toby Marlow said. He rolled his eyes heavenward. "The *highest* court."

In the outer office, the receptionist said, "The phone call, Mr. Marlow."

He fished a dime from his jacket pocket and pressed it into her soft hand.

"There's plenty more where that came from," he whispered.

He had to wait a long time for a cab. He had trouble folding himself into the back seat. In truth, he wasn't feeling so good.

"Where to, pop?" the driver asked.

That didn't help.

SCENE TWO

THE APARTMENT HOUSE on Central Park West was called The Montana. Butte should have sued. But rents were low, ceilings were high, and sometimes the elevator worked. The Marlows' apartment was on the top floor. It had four bedrooms, three baths, and closets large enough for assignations. The apartment hadn't been painted in six years; some of the walls were molting.

The cavernous living room looked like a Bolivian designer's concept of a Bavarian brauhaus. The walls were whitewashed plaster, jaundiced by age, cigar smoke, and bad jokes. Blackened beams crisscrossed the walls and ribbed the lofty ceiling. Suspended overhead was an old-fashioned, wood-bladed electric fan that turned lazily with a thoughtful hum, hardly stirring the soupy air.

At the rear was a brick fireplace, large enough to roast a cocker spaniel. There was a yellowed marble mantel, and over it hung a framed theatrical poster of Toby Marlow in the costume and makeup of Falstaff. A door at the left opened to the dining room, pantry, kitchen. The door at the right led to the entrance hall and bedrooms.

There were high windows on both sides of the fireplace. The one on the right was a bow window with a cushioned window seat. The curved bow window was fitted with leaded colored glass. Several of the small panes were broken; cardboard squares had been Scotchtaped over most of them. From one, a stuffed rag protruded.

The furniture, scaled for this barnlike room, was big, old, worn. There was an enormous couch, originally of good lines, now lumpy and sagging wearily. The velvet covering was shiny, stained, pocked with cigarette burns. Chairs were everywhere. No two matched; they all had the transient look of having come from a theatrical warehouse. They had. One had lost a leg and was propped on a tilting pile of old playscripts.

There were rickety end tables, a liquor bar on wheels, a long cocktail table in front of the couch, an old, scarred upright piano against one wall. The sheet music on the stand was "Just a Song at Twilight."

The room was further cluttered with a numbing profusion of theatrical props: a tarnished halberd with a bent blade, a plastic skull, a devil's mask, a large brass tray set with glass jewels, two burlesque bladders, a bass drum with a torn skin, fake feathers and rubber fronds, and more swell stuff. Everywhere were framed autographed photographs of obscure actors with whom Marlow had played—and some famous ones with whom he had not.

Toby Marlow, clad in a shabby, brocaded dressing gown, frayed carpet slippers, and a silk ascot of hellish design knotted awry, knelt on the window seat. He was leaning out an opened section of the bow window, screaming imprecations and flapping his arms wildly at pigeons despoiling a small terrace. Dr. Jacob Ostretter was repacking a black gripsack at the cocktail table. Blanche, the Marlows' maid, housekeeper, cook, and sergeant major, was making futile gestures at dusting and straightening the living-room thrift shop.

"Get the fuck out of here!" Marlow screamed. "Go on! Beat it!" He waved his arms, muttering. Then he closed the window, came back into the room. "Goddamn birds! They're diseased, aren't they?"

"I don't know," Dr. Ostretter said. "I've never treated a pigeon."

"Wise-ass," Marlow said. "I make all the jokes in this house. I saw your brother a few hours ago. He said—"

Jacob Ostretter threw up his hands.

"Don't tell!" he yelled. "Don't mention that man's name!"

"Julius Ostretter?" Marlow said innocently. "Nice name. It flows trippingly off the tongue."

"A gonif!" Dr. Jacob shouted. "A fiend in human form!"

Marlow laughed. "You two guys remind me of that pair from the Bible. You know..."

"Cain and Abel?" Ostretter asked.

"Don't cue me, kiddo," Marlow said. "I was thinking of Sodom and Gomorrah." He scratched his ribs and stomach. "Jesus Christ, Jake, what did you do—sprinkle itching powder under that bandage?"

"That's the incision healing."

"Healing? The hell you say. It looks like a clown's mouth."

Dr. Jacob Ostretter snapped shut his case, placed his black bowler squarely atop his pear-shaped head. But he fussed about, seemed reluctant to leave. He was a roly-poly, scarcely five-feet four with built-up heels. He lifted his plump chin and rose to his toes while speaking. He imagined it gave him a manner of stern authority. But his soft, sympathetic voice usually betrayed him. He was almost kicked out of medical school for weeping while dissecting a frog.

"Toby," he said gently, "I've got to talk to you."

"So talk."

Dr. Ostretter looked at Blanche, morosely dusting a papier-mâché owl.

"In private," he said.

Blanche started for the kitchen door.

"Horsey," Marlow said, "you take one more step and I'll give you a curettage with a Popsicle stick. Jake, whatever you've got to say, you say it in front of Blanche. I haven't had any secrets from her in thirty years, and I'm not about to start now."

Dr. Ostretter shrugged. "All right. Toby, how long have you been bleeding?"

"All my life," Marlow said.

"Don't give me any of your fancy-pantsy actors' talk. You know what I mean. How long?"

"A few years."

"How many years?"

"Four. Five. Something like that."

"Five years bleeding and you didn't come to see me?"

"I had more important things to do," Marlow said.

"More important?" Dr. Jake was shocked. "What? Tell me what?"

"Well, when it started, I was going to see you, but then I got the lead in *The Idiot*."

"Typecasting," Blanche said.

Marlow whirled on her.

"It talks!" he cried. "Jake, did you hear that? It actually talks! You get one silver star on your report card this month, honey."

"So just because you got a job, you didn't come see me?"

Marlow wandered about the room, picking things up, inspecting them, putting them down.

"The Idiot," he mused. "I was great in it, but it closed in Boston the first week. Lousy sets. The story of my life. When my time comes, I want to be taken there so they can put on my tombstone, 'He closed in Boston.'"

Dr. Ostretter shook his head in disgust.

"Can't you be serious for a minute?"

"No," Toby Marlow said.

"Well, this *is* serious. Malignant, Toby. It started in your colon. Now it's spread to the pancreas. They took one look and sewed you up. Toby, I was *there*. There's nothing that can be done."

There was silence then. The three were caught in an awkward tableau. Jake and Blanche stared at Marlow. He closed his eyes slowly. Only the derisive whir of the overhead electric fan could be heard. The moment swelled, swelled.... Then Toby opened his eyes, too much the trouper to let a stage quiet become an embarrassment.

"So much for dramatic pauses," he said. "Nothing that can be done, Jake? That's keen."

"Keen?" Blanche said. "I haven't heard that word in twenty years."

"Of course you haven't," Marlow said. "Because nothing's been keen in the last twenty years. So I'm shuffling off this mortal coil—right, Jake?"

Ostretter made a gesture.

"Yes," he said, voice breaking. "I'm sorry, Toby."

"Go to hell," Marlow said. He resumed his wandering, and Blanche resumed her halfhearted dusting. "How long do I have, Jake?"

Dr. Ostretter shrugged. "Maybe six months," he said. "Tops."

"Much pain?" Marlow asked.

"Yes," Ostretter said. "A lot. But we can help control it. You want to go into the hospital again?"

"Christ no! All those nurses had mustaches. I'll stay right here and drive everyone up the wall. I might even fuck myself to death before those six months are up."

"Wouldn't surprise me a bit," Ostretter said. "You want to consult another doctor?"

"What the hell for? I trust you. The villains with the long knives were good men, weren't they?"

"Yes, they were good men. There's no way out, Toby."

"Never has been, has there? Okay, Jake; you better send me your bill before those six months are up."

Dr. Ostretter took off his horn-rimmed glasses, wiped them carefully with his handkerchief. And with his head still lowered, he dabbed hastily at his eyes.

"I'll stop by tomorrow, Toby, and talk to you some more—about what to expect."

"I know what to expect."

The doctor moved toward the door, shoulders bowed. Then he stopped, turned back.

"Toby, have you talked to Miss Evings?"

"Barbara? Sure, I talked to her last night. Every night. She practically lives here. Why?"

"Did she tell you?"

"Tell me what?"

"I'd rather she told you."

"Tell me *what*, goddamn it? What's this all about?"

"I'll let her tell you."

"Ahh, go screw yourself. Jake . . . a lot of pain?"

"Yes. A lot of pain."

"I can stand anything but pain, hunger, and poverty."

Blanche said, "That's what make you so different from everyone else."

"See Jake?" Toby said. "She never says anything clever. I've played a hundred drawing-room comedies, and in every one of them the maid is funny as hell. But what do I get? A maid who's been playing Lady Macbeth all her life."

"I'm not your maid," Blanche said.

"Then what are you?"

"Your keeper."

"Not bad," Marlow acknowledged. "Another silver star."

"Keep on the pills, Toby," Dr. Ostretter said. "Every three hours. No drinking, no smoking, no sex. You can have sponge baths."

"Listen, Blanche," Marlow said, "maybe instead of the silver star, I'll let you give me a sponge bath."

"No, thanks," she said. "I've seen you naked before. Two prunes and a noodle."

"There you are, Jake," Marlow said. "The moment they know you're dying, the wolves close in."

The doctor shook his head dolefully, and departed through the hallway door. The moment he was gone, Toby Marlow rushed to the liquor cart and poured two whiskies. He handed one to Blanche, and set his on the cocktail table.

He then took a fat cigar from the breast pocket of his robe. He peeled off the cellophane wrapper and dropped it on the floor. He took a wooden kitchen match from a box on the table and held it high—a nonchalant Statue of Liberty. A blade of the ceiling electric fan came around, scratched across the match head and ignited it. Toby lighted his cigar, waved out the match, dropped it on the floor.

He lowered himself cautiously onto the couch,

picked up his whiskey. Blanche came over to stand in front of him. They raised their glasses in a silent toast, gulped greedily. After Marlow got his cigar drawing well, he took a deep puff, blew a series of perfect rings, handed the cigar up to Blanche. She took a deep puff, with pleasure, and handed the cigar back to him.

She was from a Nebraska farm family, and looked it. She was a big woman, with the physical presence and aggressive posture of a bordello bouncer. She was five-feet nine, weighed 158, was raw-boned, massive through the shoulders and hips, with an awesome bosom. Her wiry grey hair was pulled back tightly and tied with a girlish pink ribbon. She was pushing 60, and her features were heavy, masculine, almost equine. But the skin was unwrinkled, the complexion peachlike, even to the golden fuzz. The single gulp of whiskey had blushed not only her face, but her bare arms as well. Probably her entire strong body.

"Jake said no drinking and no smoking," she reminded Marlow.

"And no sex." He nodded. "But dying is okay."

She took another sip of the whiskey and looked at him over the glass. Their eyes locked; they stared at each other a long moment in silence.

"Scared?" she asked softly.

He took a deep breath. "'Each plays his part and has his day. What ho! The world's all right, I say.' Know who wrote that?"

"Shakespeare?"

"Jesus Christ, Blanche, he didn't write *everything!* No, it wasn't Will. I forget who the hell it was. My memory is a laundry bag of other men's words. What's for dinner?"

"Lamb stew," she said.

"Again?"

"What do you mean—again?" she demanded angrily. "We haven't had lamb stew for a month."

"That's what I mean—*again*?"

She snorted, finished off her drink, helped herself to more from the liquor cart. He held out his empty glass with an expression of such piteous pleading that she laughed and poured him more, too.

"Toby," she said, "you want me to keep it quiet?"

"The lamb stew?" he said. "Yes, I'm no prouder of it than you are. But I suppose—"

"You know what I mean," she said. "What Jake said. You going to tell the others?"

He stared at her, aghast....

"Are you out of your tiny, tiny mind? Of course I'm going to tell the others. You never supposed I'd suffer nobly and in silence, did you? Listen, sweetie, this is the fattest part I've had in five years. I'm going to pull out all the stops. I'll be magnificent: all smiling bravura on the outside, all lightness and careless gaiety that'll tear your fucking heart out. Because you'll know that deep down, inside, I'm suffering. I'll do that mostly with gestures: little controlled John Gielgud movements that will convey my unbearable anguish. God, what a performance this is going to be! How I wish the critics could catch it. I can hardly wait to get started."

"You already have," she said.

He handed her the cigar again, so she could take another puff. He inspected her through the smoke, his head tilted, eyes narrowed....

"You know, darling, you *do* look like a horse. Did I ever tell you that? Withers, fetlocks, haunch, and shank. If some day you whinnied at me, I wouldn't be a bit surprised. And yet...And yet..."

"And yet *what*, Godzilla?"

"Oh shit...I don't know. Sometimes I think that in another world, another life, another time, you and I might have been something. Something together. Something fine and beautiful. Did you ever dream of that?"

"Ohh," she whispered, "you're a devil, you are. A devil!"

He laughed and started to speak: "I suppose I—"

Suddenly he clutched his abdomen. Pain wrenched his features. His eyes rolled up into his skull.

"My God," he gasped. "Oh my God...Oh Blanche..."

She was terrified. "What is it? What is it, Toby? Should I get the pills? Should I call—"

"I'm rehearsing, for Chrissake," he said cheerfully, straightening up. "But I had you, didn't I? See how good I'm going to be when I get this part moving?" Blanche glared at him angrily. She drained her whiskey, then began again her ineffectual housecleaning. She wielded a feather duster furiously but futilely, not neglecting to dust Toby Marlow's bald head from behind, an attack he accepted with a benign smile.

For this fustian fellow was completely hairless—not even a horseshoe fringe. But his shining crown was of noble dimensions, looking like a limitlessly high brow. Far from being embarrassed by this naked pate, he gloried in its nudity, and was not above anointing it occasionally with baby oil to heighten its sheen. "This pristine globe," he called it proudly.

He had lied so often about his age that no one, including wife and son, was *quite* certain. One said 60, one said 65. *He* said 53. His complexion was ruddy, with the roadmap capillaries of a heavy drinker and the course skin texture resulting from too many years of wearing stage makeup. His nose was meaty, lips large and full, eyes wide and despicably innocent.

His voice was magnificent: deep, resonant, with a velvety vibrato—a theatre-trained voice, so even his whispers carried to peanut heaven. In spite of his age, he moved lightly, with an almost feline grace. His hands and feet were unexpectedly dainty.

Like most actors offstage, he had the appearance of

unwashed seediness. His clothes were costumes; his gestures had the outsize flamboyance of a man living his life in an arena. His favorite work of art was a mirror; if he could achieve complete androgyny, he would marry himself. Now, he sat calmly, condemned to death, lord of all he surveyed, and more, and with monumental self-assurance sipped his whiskey and puffed his cigar. His reverie was interrupted by the arrival of Barbara Evings. She floated into the room, a voluptuous wraith, bearing a nosegay of drooping violets. She embraced Blanche, kissed her cheek. Then she trotted over to the couch with bitty steps, bent to kiss Toby's bald head. She melted onto the floor at his feet, looked up, offered him the flowers.

He accepted them grandly, as his due, plucked one from the bunch to put behind his ear. He leaned forward to pull Barbara's neckline away from her body, and stared therein with a burlesque leer and a great smacking of lips. He then inserted the remaining violets between Barbara's unbra-ed breasts.

"'Weep no more,'" he recited. "'Nor sigh, nor groan,

"'Sorrow calls no time that's gone;

"'Violets plucked, the sweetest rain

"'Makes not fresh nor grow again.'"

"How do you feel today, Toby?" she asked.

"Like I've been born again."

"How wonderful!" she said. "I met Doctor Ostretter on the street. He said he had been to see you. Good news?"

Marlow turned his head away slowly, chin rising. A lofty smile curved his lips. St. Sebastian awaiting the next arrow.

"Oh, that's all right, dear," he said sadly. "Let's just talk about you."

"But, Toby, what did Jake say about you—about your condition? Are you going to be all right?"

He disengaged her arms from about his legs. He rose to his feet with some difficulty, tottered to the nearest wall. He faced it closely, pressed his forehead against it. After a two-count, he beat the wall gently with a tight fist.

"'There is no death,'" he said hollowly. "'What seems so is mere transition.'"

"Jesus Christ!" Blanche said disgustedly.

"Toby," Barbara faltered, "what are you saying?"

Marlow turned from the wall, straightened to a grand posture. With heroic gestures, he began declaiming:

"'Cowards die many times before their death; the valiant never taste of death but once. Of all the wonders that I yet have heard, it seems to me most strange that men should fear; seeing that death, a necessary end, will come when it will come.'"

Barbara, bewildered, rose to her feet. She looked to Blanche, who nodded her head. Barbara made a cry—a sob, a groan, a moan. She rushed to Toby and embraced him.

"Oh Toby, Toby, no, *no*! Say you're just joking."

"There, there, little one," he said sweetly, patting her head. "This too shall pass."

"Is it true, Toby? Are you dying?"

"It is true, dear," he said cheerily. "They cut me open and within they found such a turmoil, such a bustle of comings and goings, and little animals without number, and tissue grievously bitten. So they thought it best to sew me up again and send me home with their blessing. Go forth, they said, and sin no more. The shitheads!"

"Oh God . . . oh Toby . . . oh my God. . . ."

His orotund voice rolled out, filling the room like a Moog synthesizer:

"'There is no God stronger than death,'" he boomed, "'and death is a sleep.'"

"When?" she asked frantically. "How long do you have?"

"The end may come at any moment," he said in sepulchral tones.

Blanche headed for the door to the kitchen.

"I can't take any more of this," she said. "No bone, no fat, no water added. Just pure ham."

"Go dress like Lady Windermere," he yelled angrily after her. "Come to my bedroom at midnight and beat me off with your fan."

She thumbed her nose at him, then slammed the door behind her. Toby went over to the liquor cart, poured more whiskey, filled a glass of wine for Barbara.

"Enough of fun and games, child," he said. "Dry your tears and have a glass of sherry. 'Twill put the dimples back in your ass."

He handed Barbara the wine glass, then returned to the couch where he sat and sipped his drink, regarding her with some amusement. She stood leaning at the mantel, forehead laid upon her raised arm. With her draped dress, violets at her bosom, long black hair hanging halfway down her back, she resembled a portrait by Burne-Jones. But he would never have painted her in sneakers.

Barbara Evings hovered between girlhood and womanhood. There was something in her physical appearance that suggested she might continue to hover for the rest of her life. She was tall, thin as a breadstick, with attenuated hands and feet. Apostolic toes. Her willowy body, pliant as a stem, was usually swathed in ankle-length dresses of printed chiffon: sheer, floating stuff with ruffles, tucks, flounces—gowns that might be displayed in a museum of couturier design, hung on a mannequin of the 1920's with marcelled hair and a star-shaped mouche.

Barbara's face was smooth, untouched by age or

pain. Her light blue eyes were without guile. It was a
sweet, open face, tremulous, halfway between spiritu-
ality and insipidity. A poet might believe there was
something in those sensuous lips and that clearly
defined chin that hinted of passion and will. Something
that might one day ignite and consume her.

There was a dreaminess in her movements, a
delicacy in her manner. Naturally, she adored flowers,
birds, kittens, walking in the rain, the poetry of Indian
mystics, health food, beaded headbands, antique
jewelry, and pink babies. It was difficult to believe she
had ever been constipated.

"Barbara," Toby said, "do you have something to
tell me?"

"It isn't important."

"Doctor Jake acted like it was. So say it. Have I ever
held anything back from you?"

"No," she acknowledged, "but you're different."

"Different?" he shouted. "I'm unique! But tell me,
sweet; what's the problem?"

"I'm pregnant," she said.

"Mazeltov," he said. "But what's the problem?"

"Toby, I'm *pregnant*!"

"Thank God," he said fervently. "I was afraid it
might be an ingrown toenail. Who's the father?
David—right? My son, the actor. The actor who can't
pick his nose without asking, 'What's my motivation?'
David knocked you up?"

"Yes," she said faintly.

"It figures," Marlow said. "The clumsy oaf! The
night I went to see him in *Philadelphia Story* he
knocked over an end table. All right, honey, sit down
and let's talk about it. It's really not the end of the
world."

She returned to the couch and started to sit next to
him. But he pulled her to him so she ended up sitting on
his lap, her arm about his neck. He nuzzled his big nose
into the violets in her bodice.

"Am I hurting you, Toby?" she asked innocently, moving about on his lap.

"Ooh yes!" he breathed. "It hurts so good."

"You're a dirty old man."

"Is there a better kind? So what do you want to do? Get a free abortion?"

"They're not free, Toby. They're legal now, but not free."

"Really? I don't remember reading that in *Variety*. So you need the money—right, kid? You can't afford Doc Ostretter's fee—right? Don't worry, I'll give you the money. No problem. What will it cost?"

"Jake wants five hundred."

"Five hundred?" he screamed. "That filthy abortionist! I'll talk to him, Barbara, and for the same five hundred he'll give you a high colonic and shave your armpits. Is that what had you worried? The money? Consider the problem solved."

"No, Toby," she said. "It isn't solved. I don't want an abortion."

"Then you want to marry David?"

"No, I don't want that either."

"Whee!" he yelled.

He slid her off his lap. He staggered to his feet, pulled the robe belt tighter, fluffed his ascot. He went over to the bow window, opened a section and leaned out, looking up at the sky. Then he turned back into the room leaving the window open.

"Pardon me for about ten minutes, luv," he said. "I think I'll take a flight around the park with the other cuckoos." He stopped suddenly, put his hands on his hips. He stared down at her, frowning. "How come you're pregnant, Barbara? Aren't you on the pill?"

"No."

"Why not?"

"It seemed so—so mechanical."

"I know. Like breathing. Didn't he use anything?"

"No. I asked him not to. It seemed so—so—"

"I know—mechanical. Everything is mechanical except getting knocked up."

"Well, I believed if I thought about it, really concentrated, telling myself, 'You will *not* get pregnant, you will *not* get pregnant,' everything would be all right. I thought it was all in the mind."

"Where did he screw you—in the left ear?"

"Oh Toby," she said, "don't be vulgar."

"One of the few advantages of growing old, baby. You can be as vulgar as you like. Belch or fart, and never say, 'Excuse me.' It's beautiful. The golden years. All right, you don't want an abortion and you don't want to marry David. What *do* you want?"

She rose and came over to stand directly in front of him. She took him by the elbows and moved her face close. She stared directly into his eyes.

"I want to have the baby, Toby. I've never had anything of my own—nothing I could really love and treasure. I'll be a good mother, really I will, Toby. I'll love the baby and take care of it and protect it. I'll read books and go to classes. I *will* be a good mother, honest I will."

He took her into his arms.

"I believe you, sweetie," he said tenderly. "But I'm not sure they'll let you keep it. There may be legal complications. I'll have to talk to Julius Ostretter about that. But look, little mother, you could marry David, just temporarily, and have the baby. That would take care of the legal end. Then you could divorce him, and he'd have to provide support. How about that?"

"No, Toby. I don't want to marry David—even for one day."

"I don't blame you," he said. "But what are *your* reasons?"

She pulled from him, turned away so he couldn't see her face.

"Well. . . . David's very nice," she said in a low voice. "I like David. I love David."

"Well then . . . ?"

"Toby, it's just that I don't want to be—to be caged! I don't want to be any man's wife. I just want to be free to be myself, to own my own life."

He took her by the shoulders, turned her to him. He lifted her chin gently so she had to look into his eyes.

"You're shitting me, baby," he said.

"Yes." She nodded miserably. "I am."

"I thought you and I could talk to each other straight out, no faking."

"We can, Toby," she pleaded, "we can. But I can't talk about this. Not now."

He was silent a moment.

"Okay, kiddo," he said finally. "Whenever you're ready, I'll be here. For a while."

"Promise me you won't say anything to David about my being pregnant?"

"I promise," he said. "I won't say a word."

They heard a loud rumble of running in the hallway. The door burst open. An excited David Marlow rushed into the room.

"I got it!" he shouted. "I got it! I got it!"

"Barbara's pregnant," Toby Marlow said.

"Oh Toby," she said sorrowfully. "You promised."

"I lied," he said.

"You're looking at the world's newest Hamlet!" David Marlow laughed. "I got the job! How about that!"

"Barbara's knocked up," Toby said.

"What? What?"

"Your little Ophelia here, Hamlet. She's pregnant."

"Jesus Christ!" David cried.

"No, it's yours," his father told him.

David shook himself, a pup doused. He looked wildly about. The opened bow window appeared his only means of escape. But he was not enamored of the nine-story drop. He didn't object to the fall so much as the landing. So in his manly way, he addressed the cause of his misfortune:

"Barbara," he demanded sternly, "is this true?"

"I didn't want you to know," she said, suddenly tearful. "Toby promised he wouldn't tell."

The hallway door opened again. Cynthia Marlow came sweeping grandly into the room, arms laden with packages. She dumped them on the couch, removed her hat, shook her hair free. She went directly to Toby and kissed his bald head.

"How do you feel, Toby?"

"I'm dying," he said.

"That's nice. I'm so glad, dear. Barbara, you have new sneakers. So pretty. And clean. David, tell me—how did you make out?"

"Oh, he made out great," Toby said. "He knocked up the Bird Girl."

"I got it," David said. "We go into rehearsal on Friday. We open in six months. And Barbara's pregnant. By me. Right, Bobbie?"

"No, Judge Crater did it," Toby said.

"Toby, what do you mean you're dying?" Cynthia Marlow said. "When I came in and asked you how you were, you said you were dying. Just what did you mean by that?"

Blanche entered from the kitchen. She stood in the doorway, feet planted, balled fists at her waist, challenging. . . .

"How many for dinner?" she asked. "It's lamb stew, and I don't want to hear another word about it."

"Doc Ostretter gives me six months," Toby said.

"We'll have to get married," David said to Barbara.

"And fresh spinach salad," Blanche added.

"Toby, you must be joking," Cynthia said.

"I don't want to marry you," Barbara sobbed.

"No no no," Cynthia said, embracing Toby. "I don't

believe it. I won't believe it."

"Will you listen to reason?" David said. "Either marry me or have an abortion. One or the other."

"And a nice honeydew melon for dessert." Blanche nodded.

"What did you read for them?" Toby asked David over Cynthia's shoulder.

"'Alas, poor Yorick...'" David said.

"I *won't* marry you," Barbara said, "and I *won't* have an abortion. I'm going to have the baby—*my* baby."

Cynthia pulled away from Toby, looked at the others, appealed to the virago in the doorway:

"Blanche, is Toby telling the truth? Is that what Doctor Jake said?"

"That's what he said." Blanche nodded. "Six months."

"Oh my God," Cynthia said.

"What?" David said. "Toby dead? Six months?"

Suddenly they were all silent, staring at Toby Marlow with horror, disbelief, pity. At last, at last, he was the center of attention. He raised two fingers slowly: the Pope blessing the multitudes in St. Peter's Square. He bestowed upon them all an odiously gallant smile and whispered his benediction:

"'Weep not for me; be blithe as wont, nor tinge with the gloom the stream of love that circles home, light hearts and free! Joy in the gifts Heaven's bounty lends, nor miss my face, dear friends! I am still near.'"

"I can't stand any more of this!" David Marlow shouted. "I just can't stand it!"

He rushed from the room, slamming the door behind him.

"Go to him, Barbara," Cynthia said. "He's upset about his father."

"The hell he is," Toby said. "He's upset about *becoming* a father."

"A father?" Cynthia said. "Our David?"

"Cyn, where have you been?" Toby said. "Didn't you hear us talking? Barbara's got one in the oven, and David put it there."

"Barbara pregnant?" Cynthia Marlow said. She moved to embrace the girl. "Oh, how nice! Dear, I'm so happy for you. You're going to have it, of course?"

"Oh, she's going to have it," Toby said, "but she doesn't want to marry David."

"Why ever not, dear?"

"She's afraid he'll lock her up in a cage, or some such shit."

"What a strange idea," Cynthia said. "David would *never* do a thing like that; he's a very sweet, sensitive boy. When is the baby due, Barbara?"

"In about six months," Barbara muttered.

"Holy Christ!" Toby Marlow cried. "This house is going to be hell on wheels in six months."

"It's not doing bad right now," Blanche said. "Should I get dinner ready?"

"Might as well," Toby said. "It can't make matters any worse. Barbara, go to David's room and see if you can talk him into coming to the table. Assure him the lamb stew isn't punishment for what he's done."

"Hah!" Blanche said. "I notice you always take second helpings."

"I am your employer," Toby Marlow said loftily. "Noblesse oblige. What you don't notice, Ms. Frankenstein, is that I vomit immediately after leaving the dining room."

"You go to hell," she said hotly.

"Up yours," Marlow said.

Blanche and Barbara left the living room. Toby, finally alone with Cynthia, poured each of them a small drink.

"First today," he assured her, and she smiled wanly.

Then she slumped in a corner of the couch, leaned forward, elbows on knees. She hid her face in her hands. Toby Marlow sat beside her. He gently pried loose one of her hands, clamped her fingers around the glass.

"Over the river and through the woods," he said, holding up his glass.

She dropped her other hand, looked at him with glistening eyes.

"To grandfather's house we go," she faltered.

They simultaneously drained their shots of whiskey—a familiar ceremony—and set their empty glasses on the cocktail table. They rose, and with arms about each other's waists, moved slowly toward the door.

"I suppose we should dress for dinner," Cynthia said.

"For lamb stew?" Toby asked. "What do you suggest—sackcloth and ashes?"

He had her laughing as they went out. . . .

SCENE THREE

THE DRESSING ROOM in the Marlow apartment was actually a wide passageway between master bedroom and bathroom. One side of this rectangular chamber was wholly taken up by folding doors leading to high, walk-in closets in which Cynthia and Toby's outer clothing and shoes were stored.

The opposite wall was almost covered by the mirror of an enormous vanity table, bearing an apothecary's stock of oils, lotions, brushes, perfumes, powders, unguents, hand mirrors, colognes, combs, and makeup aids of all kinds. The table was long enough to accommodate two benches, side by side, so the mirrored table could be used simultaneously by both Marlows.

The mirror itself was a handsome sheet of beveled glass, badly in need of resilvering. Along both ends and across top and bottom ran a wooden channel in which bare electric bulbs were spaced at six-inch intervals. It was, indeed, the type of brightly lighted mirror used in theatrical dressing rooms. Even with several bulbs burned out, as they inevitably were, this blazing border provided so much illumination that further lighting of the dressing room was not needed. Not needed, but desired. Lamps shaped like spotlights were attached to the ceiling in each of the four corners. Their bright beams were aimed at the stars' benches.

Taped to the streaked mirror were withered telegrams, fan letters, photographs, jotted telephone numbers, a dried cornflower, the cover of a playbill, yellowed newspaper clippings, and similarly aged mementos of Toby Marlow's stage career. In fact, the mirror was so heavily layered with this memorabilia that only two open spaces, like portholes, remained in which Cynthia and Toby could inspect their images, an activity of which they were fond, and presently engaged.

Toby was stripped to the waist. His heavy torso was muffled in bandages, from armpits to the waist of his trousers. He looked like a wounded Buddha. Cynthia was wearing a slip, leaning forward to inspect her reflection intently as she applied makeup. Toby's study of his own phiz was no less engrossed. He stared, and sighed....

"'His life was gentle, and the elements so mix'd in him that Nature might stand up and say to all the world, "This was a man!"'"

Cynthia put aside her eyebrow pencil, turned to look at him sorrowfully.

"Poor, poor Toby," she said sadly.

"Just an average day, old girl." He shrugged. "It's the Curse of the Marlows."

"Toby, what *are* we going to do? Everything's just falling apart."

"Hang in there, kiddo," he said. "Leave everything to King Toby the First, Last, and Always. Oh, by the way—I love you, Cyn."

She smiled and reached out to stroke his bare shoulder.

"I know you do, dear—in your own strange way. You always came back to me."

"Didn't I though?" he said proudly. "Always. But of course I didn't leave you all that often."

"Often enough," she said, "often enough...."

They fell silent then, and as often happens with two people whose lives are so intertwined, their remembrance was the same. Staring at the bright lights of the dressing table, they recalled the total, hard brilliance of a Mediterranean sun....

They were on the beach at St. Tropez. The year was 1938, and bathing suits were funny. Cynthia, swaddled in something voluminous and filmy, was sitting on the sands, knees drawn up, hugging her bare feet. She was staring dreamily out to sea from under the enormous brim of a straw hat banded with a blue ribbon.

From far down the beach approached the jaunty figure of Toby Marlow. He was fully dressed in white flannels, white shirt, white cravat, white socks, white shoes, what Panama. He shone! He swung a careless Malacca, stabbing it into the sand, twirling it in complete circles, even tossing it into the air to catch adroitly and spin between his fingers.

He came up to Cynthia, quite close, and leaned on his cane, ankles crossed. He looked down at her gravely.

"I'm back," he said.

"And who might you be?" Cynthia asked coldly, not looking at him.

"I am the man with whom you are intimate."

"Oh no," she said. "No no no. The man with whom I *was* intimate—swore undying love."

"And meant it," Toby said.

They were both, in 1938, beautiful people, with the terrified self-assurance that only stage training can create. Like the well-rehearsed actors they were, they knew how this scene would end. But they had to play it out as if its climax would come as as great a surprise to them as to the audience.

"You might have written to tell me you were alive," Cynthia said. "Although I preferred to think not."

"Didn't you get the checks I sent?" he asked.

"Checks!" She laughed scornfully. "You think money absolved you of guilt?"

"Guilt?" he said. "Guilt? Guilt? What's that? The shiny stuff dancers in the Folies put on their nipples?"

"I hope she kicked you out," Cynthia said savagely.

"You know better than that. I walked away laughing."

"How old was she?"

"Nine."

"Toby, how old was she?"

"She was eighteen, but acted like nine."

"I suppose she worshiped you."

"Of course."

Cynthia made a twist of distaste, and moved so her back was to him. But he circled so he could see the tip of her nose, the point of her chin beneath the broad-brimmed hat.

"Eighteen," she repeated. "And all she wanted out of life was to be screwed by the famous Toby Marlow. That's all any of them want."

"They really don't want to be screwed by me. But they want to be able to say they have. It nourishes their egos."

"But you do it anyway."

"Why should I deny them a chance to be happy? It's such a small sacrifice to make."

"*Small* indeed!" she cried. "Undoubtedly *small*!"

"No need to get nasty about it," he said. "I did come back, you know. I always come back to you."

"Because I love you so much. Love you for what you are, with all your dirty language and evil tempers and rotten infidelities. That's why you come back to me. Not because you love me, but because you can't resist the love I have for you. I'm the only human being in the world who loves you more than you love yourself."

He was shocked by her insight. He had sensed the truth of what she said. But hearing his frailty exposed so pitilessly in words disturbed him. There were, after all, certain things a gentleman did not discuss: venereal disease, God, and the sexual proclivities of ballet dancers were three of them. His dependence on her was another.

"You know not whereof you speak," he said haughtily.

"Oh yes," she said. A derisive laugh here. "You don't love me, but only the love I have for you. I've always known it. I'm not as sexy or pretty or young as your little girls, but I love you in a way they can't. It's my only weapon."

"Well, babe," he said lamely, "it's really not such a bad life, is it? A lot of laughs to get us over the rough spots. A few little bits of happiness—enough to keep us going. Some marvelous brawls. Do you remember the time you brained me with a flowerpot?"

"Oh yes," she said. "The moment I did it I could have killed myself. It was my best African violet."

Toby laughed aloud, and Cynthia could not refrain from smiling. Finally, finally, she looked up at him. Interpreting this as a thaw, he immediately folded onto the sand alongside her and removed his Panama. He was wearing a wig of luxuriant brown hair, quite long for male styles of that day.

She inspected him critically, reached to feel his ribs.

"You're thinner," she said.

"I haven't been sleeping much."

"No, I don't suppose you have. Was she pretty?"

"In a vacuous sort of way. When she drank a cup of tea, she held up her little finger."

"Toby, she didn't!"

"She did—until one night I hung my hat on it. The tea spilled into her lap."

"You're such a brute."

"Yes. And in bed she wanted to talk baby talk. I damned soon put a stop to *that*, I can tell you."

He hitched a bit closer to her on the sand. He reached up and gently removed her hat. Then he could see her classically crisp features in profile, chiseled against an impossibly blue sky. She was aware of his stare and posed for him, lifting her chin, smoothing the long hair away from her ear.

"Oh Toby," she sighed. "*Why* do you do it? Will you tell me why? Is it *your* ego that needs young girls?"

"*My* ego doesn't need nourishing; you know that. It's because—well, I think it's because it gives me a fresh audience. You know all my lines, all my moods, tempers, passions, furies, jokes, melancholies. Cyn, you *know* me. You can't react any more. You've seen the play too often. I'm not blaming you for that. But you must understand that occasionally I need someone who doesn't know me, to whom I'm totally new, someone I can play to who *does* react, who laughs or frowns or weeps. It's like a new role for me. Does that make sense?"

"Not much," she said. "You don't have to be on *all* the time, do you?"

"Yes," he said. "I do. All the time. Then, after I've conquered this new audience of one—not in bed; that's not significant—but convinced her by my performance, made her admire me and love me, well then—then I come back to you."

"To the old, familiar audience."

"That's right. But, my God, Cyn, I'm a player. You knew that from the start. Onstage or offstage, I'm a player."

"How I wish you were a dentist."

"No, you don't. You'd be bored to tears."

"I suppose so," she sighed.

He inched closer. Tentatively he slid an arm lightly about her waist. When she didn't object, he moved a little closer. He put his lips to her ear.

"Miss me?" he whispered.

"No."

"Liar!"

He rose from the sand, walked on his knees until he was directly behind her. Then gently, he began to massage her neck and shoulder muscles, softly soothing. Gradually her head dropped forward; she sighed with contentment.

"Still at the villa?" he asked.

"Mmm-hmm."

"Rent paid for the month?"

"Mmm-hmm."

"I bumped into Mike Spigelow in Nice. He's doing a new thing for the fall season. They go into rehearsal next month. Mike thinks there's a part that's right for me. Second lead—very strong character. Lots of makeup and a heavy death scene."

"Sounds good."

"Oh yes," he said. "I think we better get back to London."

"All right," she said equably. "Anything in it for me?"

"Ahh, no," he said. "Unfortunately."

"Mike's wife going to be in it?" she asked casually.

"I believe he mentioned she is. A few lines."

"You had a thing going with her once, didn't you?"

"That was before I met you, dear."

"My, my," she said. "You were certainly a busy little boy before you met me. And you haven't slowed down noticeably *since* you met me."

"But I always—" he started.

"I know," she said. "You always come back. Just like my heat rash..."

And there they were, both remembering, back in the dressing room, older now, and both reflecting, "But no wiser." Toby was standing behind Cynthia, gently massaging the muscles of her bare neck and shoulders. Finally he left off, and went into the bathroom. He came back with a glass, holding it up to the light.

"If you don't mind toothpaste-flavored Scotch," he said, "we can share a wee bit of the old nasty."

"Did Doctor Jake say you could drink?" she asked anxiously.

"Oh sure," Toby said. "And smoke. It doesn't make any difference now."

He took a bottle of whiskey from the dresser cupboard, poured half a glass. He handed it to Cynthia who took a small, ladylike sip, and handed it back. Toby sat down heavily on his bench, took a deep swallow, stared at his image in the fogged mirror.

"Mirror, mirror, on the wall," he said, "who's the biggest schmuck of all?"

"Toby, do you think you should see another doctor?"

"No, I do not think I should see another doctor. What the hell's the point? If Jake's wrong, I'll be alive six months from now and can tell him to fuck off. But I don't think he's wrong. I saw the surgeons' reports, and—"

"Toby, you didn't tell me that."

"I didn't tell Jake that, either. You were both so

happy I came out of surgery okay, I didn't want to spoil things for you. But I bribed a nurse with a kiss and found out what the score was. Nothing to nothing. The sawbones said it had spread too much, too far..."

She reached quickly for the glass of whiskey, took a much larger gulp, shuddered, handed it back to him.

"Tastes awful," she gasped.

"I know," he said. "But it'll prevent cavities."

She turned sideways to lean on him, put her head on his shoulder, grip his arm.

"Frightened, darling?"

"Of course not. That's one advantage of being an old actor. By the time you've reached my age, you've played so many death scenes you know how it's done. I can handle it."

"*We* can handle it, love," she said.

As the many years passed, Cynthia Marlow bloomed from a rather large, plump, obviously attractive girl into a composed and tranquil woman who spoke in a musical, somewhat flutey voice in which syllable emphasis seemed to be by change of pitch rather than force of breath.

She was undeniably handsome, with splendid posture and the carriage of a minor duchess. Her fine blond hair had become more silvered than white. Combed back from a high, broad forehead, and usually gathered in a chignon, it revealed a long, soft neck. She favored collarless dresses, robes, and coats. It pleased her to accentuate Toby's raffish appearance by close attention to her own personal cleanliness and grooming. There was a warm, sweet, womanly glow to her that attracted both males and females, but especially incestuous young men searching for a mother.

Her smile was particularly radiant, and her angers rarely displayed. From her long association with Toby Marlow, she had developed the serene manner of a

practical nurse dealing with a nonviolent and frequently amusing maniac. Her eyes were an unusual
greenish brown, her nose patrician, her complexion
unmarked except for fine smile lines at the corners of
her mouth. Her body, unnecessarily girdled, was still
yielding. The plumpness of youth had become the
ripeness of middle age. She was pleased with this
change, and so was Toby.

The man himself leaned over to kiss her bare
arm....

"*We* can handle it," he agreed. "Sweet Cyn, the most
unsinful woman who ever lived. Well, luv, we have a lot
to do in the next six months. First of all, we must get
David through his rehearsals and see him open. It's just
a university theatre, but it's a marvelous chance.
Maybe a scout for porn movies will see him."

"Oh Toby," she protested, "you know you're proud
of him."

"He'll be a disaster."

"Toby, that's not fair! David shows lots of
promise."

"I wish he'd show talent."

"You can coach him, dear."

"If he'll let me," Toby said. "'How sharper than a
serpent's tooth it is to have a thankless child.' And
there's the business of Barbara's child. She wants to
have it and keep it as her very own, like some kind of
teddy bear. Just wait until she changes her first diaper
and gets crap under her fingernails. She'll change her
mind about the joys of motherhood."

"Toby, can Barbara keep the baby? Legally, I
mean?"

"I don't know. I'll have to talk to Julius about it. But
in any event, she'll need help and money. I think she
should move in here until the baby arrives—and
afterwards, too, if she likes. I don't fancy the idea of her
being alone in that Parisian garret she lives in."

"Oh Toby," she said lovingly, "you're so *kind*."

"Goddamned right," he said.

"She must move in," Cynthia said firmly. "I can make your study into a nursery."

"Screw that!" Toby shouted. "Make over David's study. He put the loaf in the stove."

"Well, we have plenty of room." She soothed him. "And Barbara will be warm and get regular meals."

"She's a health-food nut," Toby warned. "She won't eat anything that isn't grown in horseshit."

"Oh Toby!"

"It's the truth. Besides, Blanche's cooking will stunt the baby's growth."

"How can you say a thing like that?" Cynthia asked. "Blanche is a very good cook. She may not be fancy, but she has a way with plain, wholesome food like pork butts and cauliflower. And she—"

But during this encomium to Blanche's culinary skills, Toby rose and went into the bedroom. He returned in a moment, shrugging slowly and laboriously into a clean white shirt. He held out his cuffs, and Cynthia obediently put in the links.

"Now about us," he said, interrupting her monologue.

"What about us?"

"Cyn, I think we ought to get married."

"Toby!" she cried, shocked and pleased. "You're proposing!"

"Against my better judgment," he said. "Remember when Kellerman talked me into a run-of-the-play contract? I thought the damned thing was a turkey, but it ran for two years. After a while I could walk through that part dead drunk—and frequently did. I swore then—no more long-run contracts. But now I'm willing to risk it for six months. As things stand, you're my common-law wife, and I don't think there will be any trouble with inheriting. But I'd feel better if we made it all legal and nice and tidy. I know Julius Ostretter will feel better, too—bless his gnarled legal heart. Cynthia, will you marry me?"

"Well . . ." she said thoughtfully, "this isn't *quite* the way I dreamed it might happen, but the answer, darling, is yes, yes, yes!"

"I was afraid you'd say that, damn it. All right, that's settled. Now I've got to make out a will."

"Who's going to tell David?"

"That he's a bastard? I guess I'll have to. I'm not looking forward to it. 'Son, you're a bastard.' He'll probably say, 'Father, so are you.' It'll rupture my wit explaining why we never married."

"We started to a few times," she said.

"I know—but something always came up. Once I got the lead in *Much Ado*—"

"And once I got the measles."

"And once I got drunk."

"And once I lost the license."

"And once the war started."

"Yes," she said reproachfully. "And once you ran off with the belly dancer at your bachelor party."

"That diamond in her navel was a fake," Toby Marlow said.

"How do you know?"

"I tried to scratch a window with her. Well, anyway, we never got married. But better late than never. You know who said that?"

"You just did."

"If there's anything I can't stand, it's a smart-ass. For your information, my illiterate concubine, it was John Heywood who wrote 'Better late than never.' And he swiped it from Livy. Listen, Cyn, We'll have a beautiful wedding. Maybe David will be my best man."

"And Blanche can be my maid of honor," she said.

"And Barbara can be the flower girl," he said, "festooning our nuptial bed with rose petals."

"Oh yes!" she cried. "Yes! Yes!"

Toby, tucking his shirt into his pants, went into the bedroom again. Cynthia sat for a moment, chin on hand, dreaming and smiling. Not seeing her image in the aged mirror. Then she called into the bedroom, voice raised:

"Toby, did you ask Doctor Jake about sex?"

The answering shout came back:

"I asked him—but he wasn't interested."

SCENE FOUR

THE SIDEWALK along the west border of Manhattan's Central Park is paved with hexagonal slates. Some sections of the walk tilt crazily; in some, the stones are loose, cracked, or missing. Then you have your everyday, run-of-the-mill stretches where hopeful moss and stunted grass poke up between the stones. It is a city walk, demanding a wary eye for obstacles and a keen eye for dog droppings.

A stone parapet prevents pedestrians from falling into the park itself, which in several sections slopes off sharply eastward. But park trees project branches over the sidewalk, as do a line of trees set between walk and street. The result is faintly bucolic, not unlike a stage set that has become worn and somewhat tattered during the original production, and has then been taken on the road to end its days in Keokuk.

On this night the sidewalk stones were greasy with fog. Occasionally, when the clouds parted, they reflected dimly the silver paring of a quarter-moon.

The air was damp, pleasantly redolent of city smells. The wind was strong without being sharp. David Marlow wore a cardigan under his tweed jacket. Toby Marlow wore a stained trench coat and battered deerstalker cap. He was smoking an enormous cigar. After inhaling the fumes for several paces, David moved around to the upwind side for the remainder of their postprandial stroll.

Toby belched loudly.

"That lamb wasn't led to slaughter," he said. "It was chased for five miles."

David said, "You shouldn't have screamed at Blanche like that."

"And why the hell not?" Toby demanded. "I happen to love Blanche. If you can't scream at people you love, who can you scream at?"

"One of these days she'll get fed up with your tantrums and walk out on us."

"Not Blanche," Toby said. "Not a chance. She worships me. She sticks around in the hope that one of these nights I might dip Cecil in the hot grease."

"You bastard!" David said.

"You took the words right out of my mouth."

"What? What are you talking about?"

Toby turned his head and held up his hand as if he was whispering an aside to an audience. "Not yet," he said. "Not yet. The time is not ripe."

He paused under a streetlight, and David waited patiently. Toby fumbled inside his trench coat, brought out a long hammered silver flask (U.S., circa

1927). He unscrewed the top, took a deep swallow, then offered the flask to David.

"Want a douche?" he asked. "Oh, I keep forgetting your perversion: you don't touch the stuff."

"No, I don't," David said.

"No, you don't," Toby repeated. "You have other, more unnatural vices—like impregnating young girls, thou hungry, lean-faced villain."

"I offered to marry her, but she doesn't want to."

"Thus proving her intelligence and good sense."

"Dad," David sighed, "do we have to argue about this?"

"I have asked you—asked? Nay, demanded!—a million times not to call me 'Dad' or 'Pop' or 'Old Man' or 'Dad-dums' or anything but 'Toby.' My name is Tobias, of which the affectionate diminutive is 'Toby' And everyone—relatives, friends, and fans without number—is affectionate toward me and calls me 'Toby.' I extend that same right to my pigeon-livered son who has more hair than wit, and who was born under a caul when the moon was hidden, there was a weeping in the sky, and the earth trembled."

"Just what the hell are you maundering about?"

"And what's so terrible about arguing?" his father asked. "It cools the blood, cleanses the stuffed bosom of that perilous stuff which weights upon the heart, thins the bile, and clears the air. Thou clam! Thou oyster! You're so closed up that one of these days you're going to explode and splatter yourself all over the landscape."

David, convinced that his old man was finally over the edge, around the bend, and down the drain, said: "Maybe I will have a drink. A small one."

They paused again. Passersby glanced curiously as Toby took out the flask, unscrewed the cap, wiped the mouth on his sleeve, handed it over to David.

"'Wonder of Wonders, a miracle, a miracle,'" he

said. "Sip it slowly and with respect: the first big step for mankind, the first small step on the road to perdition."

David wet his tongue cautiously from the flask.

"God!" he said. "That's awful!"

"Of course it's awful," Toby said. "Did you think I've been enjoying myself all these years?"

He reclaimed the flask, took a deep swallow. They resumed their walk in silence. Occasionally they passed other strollers, dogwalkers, young couples with arms about each other's shoulders.

David Marlow was a bit over six feet tall, weighed 163. He was erect, slim, athletic, with a lightness that was part his parents' grace, part his natural musculature, and part a disciplined regimen of Yoga and dancing exercises. He had more than his father's rugged good looks, but it was an elegant beauty; his face, in repose, was almost feminine.

His hair was dark brown, silky, worn long but brushed and neatly trimmed. Brows were heavy. He shaved twice a day. This very young man had a very young mustache sprouting from his upper lip like a child's toothbrush. He had extraordinarily light blue eyes, sculpted lips, small ears set flat to the skull, teeth white and sharp. Fifty years ago he would have qualified as a "matinee idol." But he was too serious about his art to believe physical beauty an advantage; he was convinced that even if he looked like Quasimodo, he would still be destined to become the world's greatest actor.

This solemnity—about himself, his craft, his future—was reflected in the way he usually dressed: sober business suits worn with vests, white shirts, conservative ties, unwrinkled socks, and polished shoes. Verve disappeared when he stepped off the stage. Only occasionally did a warm, uninhibited laugh suggest there might be more to him than cold ambition.

His trained voice was far from being the splendid diapason of his father's, but there was good resonance to it. On occasion, it suffered from a kind of self-satisfied sonority: a corporation lawyer reading a tax brief. His gestures were artful, most of them involving the heavy black-rimmed glasses he wore offstage: whipping them off (anger), shoving them atop his head (perplexity), peering over them (disbelief), gnawing the earpiece (ratiocination). Without his glasses, he seemed ingenuous, without cunning.

"Toby..." he said.

"What?"

"Toby..."

"Are you drunk already?" his father demanded. "Instead of loosening your tongue, has that half-gram of alcohol frozen it? Now say 'Toby' just once more, and off you go to a giggle factory to dry out."

"I just wanted to tell you I'm sorry."

"Sorry?" Toby said. "About what?"

"About—about what Doctor Jake told you."

"You mean croaking? Don't be shy, thou mongrel, beef-witted loon. You won't offend me. I'm going to croak in six months. I'm going to die. Death. See? I can say it. It doesn't hurt. I've said it a hundred times in a hundred good parts, and it doesn't bother me a bit. I'm going to die."

"Well...I'm sorry."

"You know," Toby said, "you're a lousy player. Did anyone ever tell you that besides me? You-are-one-lousy-player. This is how you express sympathy—'I'm sorry'? Let me give you a short lesson, m'lad. Now you're Toby. I'm David, your son. I have just learned you're going to be dead in six months. Now get this—and *listen*, for God's sake."

The two men halted under a streetlight. Toby stepped briefly outside the circle of light, into the gloom. When he stepped back into the weak orange illumination, the transformation was startling. He seemed to have aged physically. His shoulders slumped, arms dangled helplessly, fingers trembled, knees sagged. His whole posture was one of shock and despair. When he began to speak directly to David, his gestures were more than theatrical; they were the exaggerated, distraught movements of a man staggered by an emotional cataclysm he cannot fully comprehend. His voice, ordinarily booming, had become hesitant, almost cracked with hysteria, draining away to a scratchy whisper at the end of each sentence. . . .

"Toby . . . Toby . . . I just heard. Six months? Oh my God! I wanted to die when I heard. I wanted the earth to split beneath my feet, the whole world to crack apart. Life without you? Not life, Toby, but a kind of living death for all of us. I won't—I can't—please God, say it isn't so! Toby, when you go, something will go out of my life as well, something from the lives of all of us—light and laughter and wonder and joy. We'll all die a little with you. Don't leave us, Toby. I beg of you, don't leave us!"

Almost against his will, David was conquered by this performance, fascinated by his father's technical skill, deeply moved by the emotional appeal of Toby's words.

"My God," he breathed.

"Got you, didn't I?" Toby said complacently. "As Oscar said, when it comes to sincerity, style is everything."

"Well, it's not *my* style."

Furious at himself for having been bamboozled by Toby's demonstration, David turned and began walking again, a little faster. His father hurried to catch up.

"No, it's not your style. I know your style. The method, the motivation, the introspection."

"It isn't a 'method,'" David said angrily. "Can't you

get that through your marinated brain?"

"Maybe not, but it's an approach—and the wrong approach. I never went to acting school a day in my life. I had my first walk-on at the age of six in *A Midsummer Night's Dream*. We learned from each other. We lived, ate, and slept theatre. We—"

"Oh lord, Toby," David begged piteously, "not again!"

"Yes, goddamn it, again! Walk-ons and carrying spears. Prop man and stage manager. Selling tickets and handing out programs. Burlesque and flea-bag hotels. Getting stranded and swindled on contracts. Coming into hotels through the service entrance, and what decent woman would be seen with an actor? We were rogues and renegades, thieves and seducers, whores and pimps. But now we go on TV talk shows and get knighted by the Queen. But when I started, you waded through shit to learn your art. But you *learned*. Not in any crap-ass school, but by doing! You swiped tricks from everyone you could. And you watched people, studied them. How a young boy laughed. How an old man blew his nose. How a man stabbed to death fell to the ground. How a politician swallowed his words. You learned from life. From *life,* thou arrant knave! And you learned the theatre doesn't hold a mirror up to life. Yes, it does, but it's a magnifying mirror, and everything on stage should be twice the size of life. How else can you show the wonder and sadness and humor and cruelty and madness of it? And so we, the players, must be twice the size, must be superhumans. With outsize passions and lusts and laughter. You can't walk off the stage, cold cream your face, buckle your braces, and take the midnight train to New Rochelle. Impossible! Because it's in your gut. If you have any talent at all—and I have a lot more than you give me cridit for—then you're never off. Never! You're on every minute you're awake. Your life becomes the best part you ever played."

"My God, what a gassy old windbag you are!" David said. "What a diarrhea of words! What a constipation of ideas! 'The best part you ever played.' For you, acting is playing, and actors are players. *Play*. You make it sound like a sport or diversion, a recreation or game. To you, the stage is no more than an amusement. Entertainment. Equal to baseball, backgammon, and Ring-Around-the-Rosie. And so, like the mean-souled yahoo you are, you corrupt to a craft what should be an art."

"'Mend your speed a little,'" Toby said, "'lest you mar your fortunes.'"

"'Great wits are sure to madness near allied,'" David retorted, "'and thin partitions do their bounds divide.'"

"Hmm," Toby said. "Not bad—for a wet-nosed dunderpate."

"And having debased acting from a talent to a knack, you think to master it with tricks. Your very words: 'You swiped tricks from everyone you could.' As if acting was nothing but that; the more tricks, the better actor. With your tearful winks and snuffles and shuffles and flapping eyebrows and twitches and completely irrelevant gestures and body movements. Yes, I *am* a lousy player—thank God! I cannot *play* at acting, croquet, ticktacktoe, or professional football. But I *am* an actor who respects his art and means to use it to reveal the truth."

"The truth? What truth?"

"The truth in me. But this you cannot do with your bag of superficial tricks—except to reveal your own shallowness and false pretense. Toby, you're not an actor, you're a mummer. The art of the theatre has passed you by. Most of the actors you knew and worked with would be laughed off the stage today if they appeared and ripped a passion to tatters. The theatre—"

"*Tear* a passion to tatters."

"The theatre began in great open-air arenas, and actors had to wear grotesque masks and use grand gestures to be seen and understood. Even Will's plays were done out-of-doors, the actors competing with street noise. But then the theatre moved indoors, the stage became smaller. The movie screen made it even smaller, and the TV screen smaller yet. Today acting must be closer, tighter, more disciplined, and more controlled. Not as—as *gross* as it was in your day."

"My day!" Toby shouted furiously. "My day! You whey-faced whelp!"

"In your day," David repeated inexorably. "Now we look for the motivation of a character; the appearance is not enough. We search for the significance of the speeches; the words are not enough. We're digging, digging, digging, to reveal new truths through the art of acting."

"'Young men think old men are fools; but old men *know* young men are fools.' So you're not a player, you scurvy milksop? Hah! You are, and so am I, and your mother, and Barbara, and Blanche, and so is every human being who screws and farts his hour upon the stage and then is heard no more. All you know of me and all I know of you are those 'grotesque masks' we turn to each other, the manner, the gestures, and all the little tricks of speech and movement you claim to despise. And you present a different mask, a different manner, a different character to every person you meet, and so do I, and so do we all."

David halted, drew a deep breath, whipped off his horn-rimmed glasses.

"I think I'll have another drink," he said.

"That's one trick you've swiped from me," Toby jeered.

They handed the flask back and forth. David's swallow went down easier this time. He replaced his glasses, and they resumed their walk and argument.

"Listen, you senile anachronism," David said, "are you saying we all put on an act for each other?"

"Of course, loon-boy. With everyone. And each performance is different and unique. We're all players, and we adjust to the other players, even if it's a cast of two."

"That's unadulterated bullshit! I don't play a part with you."

"The hell you don't. You've been playing Spencer Tracy when I happen to know you're Ben Turpin. I'm not accusing you of fraud or insincerity. It's just that in this lousy world, honesty would be unendurable, the final outrage. So we all try to be the player we feel the other player wants and will respond to."

"Ah, the Hero of the Geritol Generation speaks! Don't credit everyone with your hypocrisy. We're all false—is that what you're trying to say?"

"No more false than any good stage performance is false. The point I'm trying to get into your Roquefort brain is this: we all adjust the roles we play in private life to the other players in order to gain maximum response. We do this instinctively, not with malice aforethought, knowing that life, as well as the theatre, depends on communication. And that's where all your fancy theories on method acting and searching for truth fall apart. You ignore the other players, to say nothing of the audience, and make your playing a futile exercise in selfishness. Futile because all you're doing is tickling your ego. But you're not communicating. Your so-called 'acting' compares to real playing as masturbating compares to fucking. If you want to flip your daisy onstage for the rest of your life, that's your business—but don't imagine it's giving pleasure to others or opening their eyes to any great truth. Just think of how many parts you play in your private life—hundreds! thousands!—and how each role is determined by the person you're playing to, and you'll see how right I am."

"Will said it better," David grumbled.

"'All the world's a stage'? Well, Will said everything better—that son of a bitch! God, I would love to have known that man. Just to drink with him. And when he was in his cups—just tipsy, you know, but not falling-down drunk—why then he might babble. I mean, if he could write like that to make money, that commercial writing with the discipline it demands, then think of what he might say when the drink was in him, when there was no need for discipline, when he might just babble on and on, wonderful babble, whatever floated to the surface of that incredible, frightening mind. Oh, how I would have loved to share a jug with William Shakespeare and listen to him babble, the sweet, sweet man."

"I think I'll have another little drink," David said.

"Ah-ha! Getting to you, is it?"

Again they paused under a streetlight. Toby took a swallow, then handed the flask to his son. David stood a moment, holding it.

"No, it's not getting to me—and neither are you. Toby, you're living in yesterday. You're an antique."

"And you're a bastard," Toby said.

"A bastard? Because of what I said? Was that so frightening to you?"

"What you said? Oh, that was drivel. No, I mean it literally. You *are* a bastard. Your mother and I aren't married."

There was silence a moment. Then David took an enormous gulp from the opened flask. He gasped, sucked in his breath, took another deep swallow, and coughed, coughed, coughed. Toby pounded him enthusiastically on the back, and finally David recovered, shaking his head, wiping his mouth on his sleeve.

"Wow!" he said.

"Wow?" Toby asked. "Would you explain the motivation of that 'Wow' to me? The hidden significance? The real truth?"

"Why didn't you get married?" David demanded.

"Oh..." Toby said casually, "we never got around to it."

"Why are you telling me now?"

"We've decided to get married before I die. I'd like you to be my best man."

David stared at him, about to explode and splatter himself all over the landscape. But finally he removed his glasses again and collapsed in helpless laughter, ending with what sounded suspiciously like a drunken giggle. Finally, when he was able to speak...

"I like you, sir. I do indeed. You are an original, sir. An original!"

"Who the hell is that supposed to be?" Toby asked.

"Sydney Greenstreet in *The Maltese Falcon*."

"It stinks. Here's the way it should be done: 'I like you, sir. Mmm, you are an original. You are that, sir.'"

And, in truth, his impersonation was much better than David's.

"So..." David said, drawing a deep breath. "Going to make an honest man out of me, are you?"

"Something like that."

"How does it feel to be the father of a bastard?"

Toby looked at him a long moment. "You should know. How *does* it feel to be the father of a bastard?"

Realization was slow in coming. Then...

"Oh Jesus!" David said in a shocked voice. "I forgot about Barbara. What are we going to do about that?"

"Oh-ho, now it's 'we,' is it? 'What are *we* going to do about that?' Well, issue of my loins, I will make you a very generous offer. I will either marry your mother or the mother of your child. Is that not a fair offer? Can I possibly do more?"

"Yes," David said. "Go fuck yourself."

"Good," Toby nodded. "Excellent. I'm beginning to think there may be more than Drano surging through those clogged arteries of yours."

David was still disbelieving. "I'm really a bastard?"

"I've been telling you that for years."

"And you're really going to marry Mother before you—before you—"

"Before I croak?"

"Yes. Before you croak."

"I am indeed," Toby said. "A marvelous ceremony. In Technicolor, wide-screen, with a cast of thousands. You may invite as many as you wish—especially from your acting class. Let them get a final look at what it means to be a player."

"Don't start that again."

"Not only will I start it," Toby said, "but I shall continue it until I pry some sense into that mass of Play-Doh you call your brain. When do your read-throughs begin?"

"On Friday."

"Got the lines?" Toby asked.

"Not too well."

"Get the lines. The lines! Then we'll start working."

"You never played Hamlet, did you?"

"No, but I did Claudius twice and Polonius three times. I know that script better than you'll ever know it."

"I've got some great ideas for it," David said.

"Forget your ideas," Toby advised. "Will had them long before you did, and his are better."

"How come you never played Hamlet?"

Toby Marlow was silent a moment, then said, "It's getting late. We'll go back now."

David upended the flask and drained it. Then, giggling, he shook it upside down to prove it empty. He handed it back to Toby, who also shook it upside down, looking at it sorrowfully.

"Oh, what a generous slob art thou!" he said. "'A woman would run through fire and water for such a kind heart.'"

They turned about and began to retrace their steps. But David was staggering a bit, stumbling, making heavy going of it. Finally Toby put an arm about his son's shoulders, half supporting him.

"Lissen, Toby..." David said. "Lissen...'s wise son knows his own father."

"Thank you, Henry Wadsworth Longfellow. Ask Barbara to stay with us. To move in. She shouldn't be alone, and we have plenty of room. Your mother and I want her to stay. And Blanche loves her."

"All ri'." David nodded wildly. "I'll tell her."

"Don't tell her, ask her."

"All ri', all ri', I'll ask her. Toby... Toby, I'd marry that woman tomorrow if she'd jus' say yes."

"Forget it. She won't."

"Jus' say yes. One little yes."

"Are you drunk?" Toby asked incredulously. "On what must be at least two ounces of blended Scotch?"

"Not drunk," David protested vehemently. "Not drunk 'tall. Feel li'l—li'l light-headed."

"And tomorrow, after you sober up, you'll still be light-headed. I can see your reyiews now: 'David Marlow played Hamlet. Hamlet lost.'"

The two, father and son, linked together and sharing their staggers, dwindled away through the gloom, lurching from side to side, occasionally trading insults, spouting quotations of no particular relevance, and sometimes breaking into fragments of song. Their voices were surprisingly harmonious, but passing pedestrians were careful to give these roistering clowns a wide berth. Eventually, they disappeared in the fog....

SCENE FIVE

THE MARLOWS' BEDROOM was a high-ceilinged, squarish chamber dominated by an enormous four-poster bed, complete with fringed canopy. The entrance was from the left. An archway at right led to the mirrored dressing room and bathroom (decorated with circus posters).

This room was large enough to accommodate four chests of drawers placed between five curtained, floor-to-ceiling windows.

There was an oval, glass-topped table set around with chairs, used for breakfasts and occasional late suppers. A damask-covered chaise longue was positioned near the windows. There was a heavy leather club chair with a drum table alongside. The table bore a green-shaded student lamp on its scarred and pitted top. Concealed within the cabinet was a small cellaret. A marble-topped commode and a bedside table, with telephone, completed the room's heavier furnishings.

But like the living room, this sleeping chamber was a hodgepodge of theatrical props, mementos, framed photographs, souvenirs, and, oddest of all, a little one-word sign of red neon tubing set on a special stand. At the moment, this sign was switched on and was flashing "Marlow... Marlow... Marlow..." at regular and hypnotic intervals.

Toby Marlow was properly costumed for sleep, wearing a long linen nightshirt and nightcap with a tassel ball hanging rakishly over his right ear. His feet were bare. He stood near the oval dining table. There was a bowl of fresh fruit on the table, and Toby was dexterously juggling three oranges and an apple. He was glancing about indifferently—but really waiting for the applause to start.

Cynthia, in flowing nightgown and negligee, was stretched out on her side on the chaise longue. She was engaged in a complex series of languid, preslumber exercises that included patting gently beneath her chin with the back of her hand, moving her head slowly about on her neck, opening her mouth wide in a strained and frightening grimace, etc.

Blanche, wearing an old flannel robe over her flannel nightgown, her hair in curlers, was engaged in a housekeeping chore: changing the linen on the Marlows' bed. Neither she nor Cynthia glanced at Toby's juggling feat; they had seen it many times before. Finally, unappreciated, Toby replaced the oranges in the fruit bowl and began wandering about the room, munching on the apple.

"Well," he said, "I told him."

"That's nice, dear," Cynthia said.

"How did he take it?" Blanche asked curiously.

"All right," Toby said shortly. "The kid's all right." Then he turned, threatening: "But don't tell him I said so."

Blanche laughed. "God forbid that anyone might think you were human."

Still wandering, still gnawing on his apple, Toby stopped at the bedside phone and pointed.

"Look at that goddamn phone. It never rings. It just *never* rings. I've been in plays where the phone rings every ten minutes. That's how you learn your rich uncle just died and left you a million dollars, or your wife ran away with the butler, or with your mistress—or whatever. But our phone never rings. Damn it, doesn't *anything* work in this house?"

"You sure as hell don't," Blanche said.

"You're really asking for it, kiddo," Toby said. "Keep on like that, and you'll earn a swift kick in the cruller. I'm bigger than you are."

"The bigger they are, the harder they fall," said Blanche.

"Don't you believe it," Toby said. "The bigger they are, the harder they kick. Listen, will you stop caressing my sheets and get the hell out of here? I want to seduce my wife."

"She's not your wife," Blanche said, turning down the comforter and patting it.

"Perhaps not at this point in time," Toby said, all haughty dignity. "But she is the woman with whom I share connubial bliss."

Both women had a fit of the giggles, and Toby looked at them suspiciously.

"I don't like the way you two witches have been acting lately," he said. "There's something going on. A conspiracy. Against me."

"Oh Toby!" Cynthia said.

"It's true. Two witches. If there was one more of you, you could play *Macbeth*."

"And if you weren't so bald," Blanche said, "you could star in *The Hairy Ape*."

"And you could star at Epsom Downs just the way you are," Toby retorted. "Don't ever try to top me, horsey. It can't be done."

Blanche made a lewd gesture toward him, middle finger extended. And then laughing inaudibly, she exited and closed the door behind her. Toby finished his apple, tossed the core into the bowl of fresh fruit. Then he shuffled over to the freshly made bed and sat down heavily. Cynthia looked at him anxiously.

"How do you feel, Toby? Truly."

"Truly? Not so good. A little weary. It's been a heavy day. I think I'll lie down and take a little nap till morning."

"A very good idea," Cynthia nodded approvingly. "I'll be along in a minute."

"I don't think I'll be able to get it up tonight."

"You always say that, but you always do."

"With a little help from my friends."

Toby slowly straightened out on his side of the bed, pulled the comforter over his legs. Cynthia rose and moved about the room, taking his apple core from the bowl of fresh fruit and dropping it into a waste basket, opening windows, adjusting curtains, etc. Toby's eyes followed her as she moved.

"Cyn, did I tell you I loved you?"

"Yes, you did." She smiled. "That's twice in one day."

"I might even say it again. That'll be three times—a new world's record."

"In one day!" Cynthia exclaimed.

She came over to the bed, sat near him. He moved over a bit to make room for her. She took up his hand, kissed the fingertips.

"Tastes of apple," she said. "Toby . . ."

"What?"

"Will everything be all right? Tell me everything will be all right."

"Stick with me, kid, and you'll be wearing diamonds."

They smiled, looking at each other, remembering the first time he had told her that. The first time they met . . .

It was a cramped, rather ratty backstage dressing room. The ceiling was low, the paint on the walls leprous, the furnishings old without being quaint. The light came from a single naked bulb hanging from an overhead wire and from a border of low-wattage bulbs surrounding a dressing table much smaller and infinitely more tatty than the grand mirror in the Marlows' present dressing room.

The year was 1932. Toby Marlow was scoring a personal success as the leading juvenile in a dreadful musical comedy called *Please Don't, Sophie*! It had already played two nights and would play two more before dying a merciful death, hurried along by a respected critic who wrote, among other things, "The sex in this alleged 'comedy' makes me want to set fire to every bed in the world."

But Toby's notices had been very good indeed, and he had every right to the complacent smile he exchanged with his reflection in the dressing-table mirror as he removed his stage makeup. He was stripped to the waist, his torso still sweated from the final frantic and hopeless dance scene. Even his bald pate gleamed with moisture. Toby wiped it dry with a distressingly soiled towel.

Suddenly there was a sharp, peremptory knock on the dressing-room door. . . .

A male voice shouted, "Mr. Marlow! Someone to see you. Are you decent?"

"Just a minute," Toby yelled.

Hastily he pulled on a wig, adjusted it carefully, patted it smooth.

"Entrez vous!" he caroled. Then, when there was no answer, no reaction, he screamed, "Come in, come in, goddamn it!"

As he spoke the last line, Toby rose to his feet, took two strides to the door, yanked it open angrily. He thawed immediately when he saw what fortune had brought him: a soft, uncorseted, pretty young woman. She was trembling with nervousness, holding a single red rose awkwardly.

"Well well well," Toby said. "What have we here?"

Faltering at first, then in a rush to recite the speech she had obviously rehearsed, the young woman said, "Mr. Marlow, I just wanted to tell you I think you're the greatest actor ever, and I've seen the play both nights, and it's a terrible play, and the only reason I went was to see you, and I wanted you to know and and to have this."

She thrust the rose at him. He accepted it gracefully with a tender smile.

"Bless you, child—son of a *bitch*!"

He shook his hand furiously, then sucked at his thumb.

"Oh dear!" she said. "I guess I should have removed the thorns."

Toby smiled bravely.

"'The heart that is soonest awake to the flowers is always the first to be touched by the thorns.' Do come in, darling. It was very sweet of you to visit me."

He ushered her into the dressing room, closed the door and, while she was looking about, locked it furtively.

"Not very palatial, is it?" he asked cheerily. "Sit over here in this chair. But do be careful of that right rear leg; it has a tendency to collapse. How did you manage to get past the stage door? Bribe?"

"Oh no. Mac and I are old friends. I played this theatre once."

"Did you now? In what?"

"Well...it was just a Christmas pantomime. I played a canteloupe."

"A canteloupe? Juicy part!"

They both laughed. Toby was excited by the way she laughed: head thrown back, throat strong and full. He pulled his wire-back chair over to face her. He sat down, still holding the rose gingerly. He moved his chair so close their knees were almost touching.

"What is your name, dear?"

"Cynthia Seidensticker. But I use the name Cynthia Blake."

"I should think so! Cynthia is a beautiful name. I love the sound of it. I could do a lot with 'Cynthia.' For instance: Angry: 'Cynthia!' Imploring: 'Cynthia?' Passionate: 'Sss-Cyn-the-aaah.'"

"You're just marvelous!"

"Oh yes," he said. "And what else have you done—on the stage, I mean?"

"Well—uh—I did a season of summer stock in the States."

"You're lying, of course?"

"Of course."

Again they both laughed, and Toby hitched his chair even closer to her. Cynthia couldn't seem to take her eyes from his wet torso.

"You're all perspired," she said faintly.

"Sweaty. Lords perspire; actors sweat. Be a luv and wipe me down, will you?"

He stood, tossed the rose aside. He held the soiled towel out to her. Hesitantly she stood up, took the towel, began to wipe his turned back gently.

"I'm really not a very good actress," she confessed.

"I'd like to be, but I'm not."

"Then forget about the theatre," Toby advised. "It's no place for doubt."

"But I love it," she said, wiping away busily.

"Good. Buy tickets then. Married?"

"No."

"Lover?"

"No."

"Boy friend—or friends?"

"A few," she said hesitantly. "Nothing serious. But I don't know why I'm telling you all this. You can't be interested."

Toby turned to face her. She continued wiping his neck, shoulders, chest, and ribs with the sodden towel, engrossed in her work. Young Toby had an impressive torso, firm and gracefully muscled. He took the towel from her trembling fingers, dropped it to the floor. He clasped her upper arms softly.

"Of course I'm interested," he said. "You're very lovely, Cynthia."

"Thank you."

"'Cynthia, fair regent of the night.'"

"What's that from?" she asked.

"I don't know. Something that sticks in my mind." Gently, hands still on her upper arms, he pulled her toward him until she was pressed against him. Her head bent back fearfully.

"Cynthia," he whispered. "Do you know what the name 'Cynthia' means?"

"What?" she said, breathless now.

"She who seeks love."

"You're—you're making that up... aren't you?"

"Yes, but that doesn't make it a lie. Does it?"

She was silent.

"It's not a lie, is it?"

"No," she said faintly.

He moved a hand behind her head, pressed her face close to his.

"'Then come kiss me, sweet and twenty;

"'Youth's a stuff will not endure.'"

"Oh, I couldn't, Mr. Marlow," she said. "I just
couldn't!"

"'They do not love that do not show their love.'"

He pushed his mouth against her closed lips. She
stared at him with widened, shocked eyes. He withdrew
his opened mouth.

"'The kiss you take is better than you give.'"

"Please don't, Mr. Marlow. I didn't—I just—this is
all wrong."

"'To do a great right,'" he quoted, "'do a little
wrong.'"

He kissed her again. This time she melted against
him, her mouth open. But her eyes compensated for it
by closing. Then, breathing heavily, she pulled away. A
little.

"'Love goes toward love,'" he whispered.

"I want to leave here this instant," she said loudly. "I
want—"

"'Speak low,'" he urged, "'if you speak love.'"

"What makes you think I want you to make love to
me? How dare you—"

"'I dare do all that may become a man; who dares do
more is none.'"

"You're the most conceited person I've ever met.
Just because I—"

Again he kissed her, and again she melted. His slow
hands moved over her shoulders, down her back,
across her ass. Then, with tender fingers, he touched
her face.

"'There's language in her eyes, her cheek, her lip.'"

"Please don't, Mr. Marlow, I beg of you. I've never
done anything like this before. I will *not* do it. I shall
scream for help."

"'The brain may devise laws for the blood.

"'But a hot temper o'er leaps a cold decree.'"

"Have you no shame, sir? No shame at all?"

"'The lady doth protest too much, me-thinks.'"

"And me-thinks you are a cad and a—uh—bounder. You are certainly no gentleman. Doesn't my virtue mean anything to you?"

"'Some rise by sin, and some by virtue fall.'"

Again they kissed, more warmly this time. Their arms curved about each other, pulled sweetly close.

"I'm going to cry," she said.

"'Love comforteth like sunshine after rain.'"

"No no no! Can't you understand what 'no' means?"

"'Have you heard it fully oft,

"'A woman's nay does stand for naught.'"

He took up one of her hands, pressed the opened palm to his mouth.

"What are you doing?" she cried.

"'To kiss the tender inward of thy hand.'"

"Oh..." she said dreamily. "Oh...Your tongue drives me wild."

"'Her voice was ever soft, gentle, and low, an excellent thing in woman.'"

He fumbled at the top button of her blouse, but so intense was his excitement that he made a sorry job of it. She attempted to help him, but their fingers became entangled as their efforts grew increasingly frantic.

Toby was furious. "'The attempt and not the deed confounds us!'"

"Here," she directed, "take your hands away and let me do it. There's a button *and* a snap."

Obediently he dropped his hands to her waist. After a moment she succeeded in opening the top fastening.

"'Let me take you a buttonhole lower,'" he said eagerly.

He unbuttoned the front of her blouse and spread it wide. He caressed the tops of her breasts bulging from her chemise.

"Oh...Oh, Toby..."

"'A dish fit for the gods!'"

"Where can we...? Is there a...?"

He kicked a chair out of the way, sank to his knees on the dusty floor, reached up for her.

"'Come unto these yellow sands and then take hands.'" She sank down alongside him. They kissed again, only their lips touching as their maddened fingers ripped at buttons, hooks, belts. They paused a moment, half-naked, to catch their breath.

"'Give me your hand,'" he said, "'and let me feel your pulse.'"

"Oh Toby, your skin's so smooth. You're so beautiful."

"'Love looks not with the eyes but with the mind,

"'And therefore is winged Cupid painted blind.'"

He slipped the straps of her chemise from her shoulders, tugged it gently down to her waist. In the fashion of that day, she was wearing a bandeau, and reached around to her back to unbutton it. Unfettered, her naked breasts swelled out, nipples already engorged. Toby swooped...

"'Where the bee sucks, there suck I.'"

He lipped and tongued her faintly veined breasts, then drew his mouth away with a soft plopping sound. He touched the tumescent flesh.

"'As smooth as monumental alabaster.'"

"We must undress," she gasped. "We must be completely *bare*!"

"'I never knew so young a body with so old a head.'"

They disrobed each other, not in frenzied haste, but not wasting any time either. Then they were both nude, lying on their sides atop their crumpled clothing. They stroked, almost timorously.

"'The naked truth,'" Toby said.

"How lovely!" she breathed. "How delightful! Why have I been denying myself?"

"'Lady, you are the cruellest she alive

"'If you will lead these graces to the grave

"'And leave the world no copy.'"

"Oh heavens! How silky his ass is!"

"'There's a divinity that shapes our ends

"'Rough-hew them how we will.'"

They explored each other's bodies with hungry mouths, grasping hands, prying fingers. Cynthia ran her lips across Toby's ribs.

He said: "'Love's best habit is a soothing tongue.'"

She blew warm breath upon his belly and groin, then fluttered her eyelashes lightly over his skin.

"'The fringed curtain of thy eye advance!'"

She grasped his penis in her hot fist.

"What a glorious twitcher!" she exclaimed.

"'A very gentle beast, and of good conscience.'"

She moved it to her mouth and sucked thoughtfully.

"'O! that way madness lies; let me shun that.'"

"Don't you like me to do it?"

Toby stroked her hair tenderly.

"'What's mine is yours, and what is yours is mine.'"

Promptly he moved around until his face was at her feet. He inspected closely.

"'Toes unplagu'd with corns.'"

He popped her toes into his mouth. She squirmed with pleasure.

"We are mad! Toby, we are mad!"

"'If this were played upon a stage now, I could condemn it as an improbable fiction.'"

His nibbling mouth moved over her naked calves, behind her knees, up her soft thighs.

"Oh..." she moaned. "Oh..."

"'As chaste as unsunn'd snow.'"

"Oh my dear, I think I shall die. Or at least faint. What are you going to do next?"

"'I'll tickle your catastrophe,'" he said.

"Heavens, I'm all wet."

Toby turned her onto her back, lifted her knees high and spread them. His face delved between her thighs, and he peered at her softly furred vulva.

"'Tis not so deep as a well, nor so wide as a church door; but 'tis enough; 'twill serve.'"

He buried his face in her, his lips, tongue, yea, even his teeth busy with his passion.

He gasped: "'A very ancient and fish-like smell.'"

"Brute!" she said. "Can we do it now? Please, Toby, do it now. Any way you like. How shall we do it?"

"'Commit the oldest sins the newest kind of ways.'"

Toby rose to his knees, Cynthia to hers. Both kneeling, backs straight, they faced each other and embraced. They kissed, mouths wide and working.

"What fun!" she cried.

"'Keep a good tongue in your head.'"

Cynthia drew away, sat back on her heels, regarded him gravely. She drew smooth palms down his torso, encircled his stiffening halberd with gentle fingers.

"There is something I must tell you, dear Toby. I am a virgin. I've never done it before. Does that spoil everything?"

"'An unlesson'd girl, unschool'd, unpractised,

"'Happy in this, she is not so old but she may learn.'"

"Will it hurt?" she asked anxiously.

"'The pleasing punishment that women bear.'"

"Oh darling, darling..."

"'When love speaks, the voice of all the gods

"'Makes heaven drowsy with the harmony.'"

"Do you love me, Toby?"

"'Talkers are no good doers.'"

"Can't you say you love me—just once?"

"'Men of few words are the best men.'"

"All right," she said, "I'll twist it off."

She mangled his poniard dreadfully, flicking it, snapping it, threading it through her fingers. Then she leaned forward to munch on it hungrily. He groaned....

"'Do you think I am easier to be played on than a pipe?'"

"I'll bite it off!" she vowed.

He panted: "'Do not give dalliance too much rein!'"

She dropped her hands and watched with wonder and delight as his stiletto became a scimitar, swelling and throbbing, empurpled and nodding at her.

"Heavens," she said, "how it's changed!"

"'This is the short and long of it.'"

"Oh Toby, do it now. *Now*, Toby!"

She leaned forward on her knees again, pressed close, hugged him tightly.

"'Eyes, look your last!'" he shouted. "'Arms, take your last embrace!'"

She reached up to stroke his hair. Before she could touch it, he cried . . .

"'If you have tears, prepare to shed them now!'"

. . . and snatched off his wig. He tossed it onto the dressing table, a dead pelt. Cynthia laughed and caressed his bald pate, then pulled it down to kiss it. Toby arranged her, and she docilely allowed herself to be moved into positon on her spread knees, forearms flat on the floor, head down between her hands, rump up and sprung. Her cheek was on the floor, her hair flung wide. Toby knelt behind her. His hands followed her narrow waist, the mellow flare of her hips. Then his fingers sought and found the opening to her purse. He rubbed swiftly.

"Don't tease," she begged. "Please don't tease!"

"'I must be cruel, only to be kind.'"

"I want you *in* me!"

He looked down at himself with astonishment . . .

"'Is this a dagger I see before me, the handle toward my hand?'"

He grasped his rigid bilbo. He leaned forward. He thrust it home.

"Ahh!" she wailed. "Ahh! Ahh!"

"'A hit!'" he screamed. ""A very palpable hit!'"

"How sweet! How glorious! How lovely! How sublime! What must I do, Toby? Tell me what to do."

Toby: "'Play out the play!'"

He pressed tightly to her. Imprisoned, he put his hands upon her hips and moved them about. In circles, squares, heptagons, quattuordecillions, and other geometric forms. Including spirals.

"Oh..." she moaned. "Oh...I am burning up."

"'A little pot and soon hot.'"

Cynthia's gyrations became more excited. Now her entire body was caught up in the rhythm of her pleasure. She no longer needed his professorial hands.

"'Though she be little,'" he said. "'she is fierce.'"

"Must you make jokes about it?" she demanded.

"'How oft when men are at the point of death, have they been merry.'"

Cynthia, carried away by her quick mastery of this new art, became too ferocious in her efforts, and Toby was dislocated.

"Sorry, dear," she said.

"'The course of true love never did run smooth.'"

"I'll go slower."

"'More matter and less art.'" he urged.

Cynthia's movements became more subtle, and the two worked away with a right good will, giving each other gladness and exchanging such pleasantries as moans, groans, gasps, and expiring sighs.

"Don't leave me now!" she entreated.

"'I'll not budge an inch!'"

"Faster! Deeper!"

He puffed: "'Can one decree too much of a good thing?'"

"I feel...I feel...Don't stop! Toby, I beg you, don't stop!"

"'A man can die but once.'"

Their joy became more intense until, bursting, a final jolt exploded them both.

"Bliss!" she expired. "Bliss!"

"'O, amiable, lovely death!'"

Still joined, the two-backed beast, they coupled compulsively in diminishing rhythm.

"I come, I come," she said dreamily. "I drown, I drown."

"'Great floods have flown from simple sources.'"

Their bodies shuddered to a halt. Without strength, without sense, they collapsed, stretched out flat. Both were face down, Toby lying on Cynthia's back. He was still within her. Just. Their breathing eased, heartbeats slowed.

"I never knew," she murmured "I never knew. Perfection."

Toby: "'I'll tell the world.'"

Cynthia fumbled between her legs, then looked at her fingers....

"And I'm not even bleeding!"

"'All's well that ends well,'" he said.

"Let's do it again!"

"'What?'" He laughed. "'Wouldst thou have a serpent sting thee twice?'"

Gently he disengaged himself from her, rolled off, sat on the floor. She too sat up, close to him. They looked down sadly at his blunted lance.

"Oh dear..." she mourned. "Did I do that?"

"'O, withered is the garland of the war!

"'The soldier's pole is fallen.'"

"But you liked it, didn't you, Toby?"

"'I may justly say, with the hook-nosed fellow of Rome, I came, I saw, I overcame.'"

Lying on the dusty floor, they embraced and spent a time kissing quietly and whispering nonsense. Then there was a hard, demanding knock on the dressing-room door.

"Mr. Marlow," a voice demanded, "are you decent?"

Toby looked questioningly at Cynthia. She nodded happily. He swooped to bestow a kiss of benediction on her thicket.

"We're locking up, Mr. Marlow," the offstage voice continued. "You've got to leave now."

Toby grumbled. . . .

"'Cursed be he that moves my bones.''

Cynthia and Toby Marlow, smiling and nodding, were back in their bedroom in the apartment on Central Park West. There was faint illumination from the five tall windows. The chandelier and lamp had been turned off, but the red neon sign flashed endlessly "Marlow . . . Marlow . . . Marlow . . ." The forms of Cynthia and Toby were dimly apparent in their canopied bed.

"I remember," Toby said. "And then I took you to the Savoy for supper."

"Where I paid the bill," Cynthia said.

"Did you?" Toby said. "Well, it was the least you could do after what I had done for you."

"I agreed completely—at the time. And it was after supper that you said, 'Stick with me, kid, and you'll be wearing diamonds.' I didn't know then it was a joke; you were just quoting from some awful book or movie."

"Well, it was a joke and it wasn't. It was a half-joke."

"And you half-meant it," she said. "Then we walked home to that dreadful hotel where I was staying."

"And you wouldn't let me come up," he recalled.

"That's right. I said it was too late at night, and do you remember what you said then?"

"What did I say?"

"It was your last quotation of the evening. You said, 'It is not night when I do see your face.' That was so dear, so dear."

"That's true." He nodded.

"You meant *that*, didn't you, Toby? Are you falling asleep, darling?"

"Mmm... getting there. Hold me."

"Like this?"

"Yes. Good night, dear love."

"Good night," she said tenderly. "Good night, good night..."

There were a few moments of silence, dim movement on the bed, then springs creaking...

"Cyn..."

"What is it, darling?"

"Cyn, I forgot to say my prayers."

"Oh Toby, you haven't said your prayers in forty years."

"Well, I want to say them now."

"Then *say* them, dear."

Silence again; a short pause.

"Cyn..."

"What is it now?"

"Will you say my prayers for me?"

"Whatever for?"

"Well... I think they'll carry more weight coming from you."

"All right, Toby. I'll say your prayers for you."

He was satisfied, and snuggled down, hugging her.

"Thank you, Cyn. Give a good performance, will you?"

Finally, they slept. But the neon sign continued to blink: "Marlow... Marlow... Marlow..."

ACT TWO

SCENE ONE

THE OFFICE OF Julius Ostretter was on 58th Street,
opposite the Plaza. Julius was the Marlows' attorney
and brother of their family doctor, Jacob Ostretter.
His chambers would serve as a stage set for any
successful lawyer's office: couch and chairs of mahog-
any, with dark green leather and brass nailheads. There
were framed diplomas and licenses on the walls, a worn
but good Oriental rug on the parquet floor. There were
glass-fronted cases of law books, an enormous but
faded globe within a walnut stand, a small table
bearing a thermos of ice water and four glasses (turned
down) on a silver tray.

On Attorney Ostretter's imposing desk was a tinted photograph of his wife; phone and intercom; sharpened pencils arranged precisely along the edge of an oversized desk blotter with corners of black alligator, the same leather that adorned a rocker blotter, the handle of a letter knife, and a heavy penholder.

At the moment, this neat, organized desk was littered with stacks of dog-eared papers, some yellowed with age; an ancient ledger, the binding broken and mended with tape; several smaller notebooks; bankbooks; bond and stock certificates; and the like....

Cynthia Marlow was seated comfortably in a club chair in front of the desk. She was knitting placidly on what appeared to be a 40-foot scarf of fire-engine red, the wool coming from a shopping bag at her feet.

Toby Marlow, clad in grey flannel slacks, an open-necked shirt with carelessly tied cravat, and a sport jacket of shocking plaid, was, unaccountably, practicing dance steps. He was moving about the room in slow pirouettes and crouches, the aged ballet dancer, arms waving languorously, legs lifting and drifting downward. He was making no sound, moving to a music that only he could hear. But there was a pleased smile on his face and, indeed, there was grace and happiness in his solo dance.

The only sounds, other than the click of Cynthia's knitting needles, came from Julius Ostretter, seated in the heavy swivel chair behind the desk. Funereally dressed, steel-rimmed spectacles set firmly in place, he was reading slowly through some of the tattered papers on his desk blotter. He refused to look at Toby's ridiculous antics.

"Mm-hmm," he mm-hmmed. "Mm-hmm. Mm-*hmm*."

"Cynthia, luv," said Toby, "have you ever heard more meaningful dialogue in your life? 'Mm-hmmm. Mm-hmm. Mm-*hmm*.' David could do wonders with that—if someone told him his motivation."

Julius finally looked up and slapped the pile of papers with his palm.

"Mr. Marlow, I must—"

"Your brother Jake calls me Toby."

"Please don't mention that disgusting creature's name in my presence!"

"I beg your pardon," Toby said humbly. "A certain physician, who shall be nameless here, addresses me as Toby. He has ministered to the physical needs of my family for many years. You have devoted your considerable legal talents on our behalf for a similar number of years. Could you not—in the kindness of your shrunken, juridical heart—address me as Toby? I, in grateful return, shall call you Julie."

"It's not professional," the attorney said. "I prefer 'Mr. Ostretter.'"

Toby sighed heavily.

"'The first thing we do,'" he said to Cynthia, "'let's kill all the lawyers.' King Henry the Sixth, Part Two, Act Four, Scene One."

"Scene Two, dear," she said placidly.

"Tell me, Mr. Marlow," Ostretter said, "this is a complete declaration of all your assets?"

"Except for my genius," Toby said. "Yesterday Cynthia and I made the perilous journey to our safe deposit box in a downtown bank. There we retrieved all that crap on your desk."

"And I typed out the inventory on David's typewriter," Cynthia said brightly. "With two carbons. Messy job. I just *can't* get the black off my fingers."

"Tell me, Julie," Toby said, "have you ever been in a safe deposit vault?"

"I have. Of course I have."

"Those little rooms they give you, where you take your box. And you can lock the door from the inside. Cynthia and I thought we might screw in there."

"I beg your pardon?" the lawyer said.

"That cute little room," Toby said. "With a small glass-topped table, scissors, rubber bands, paper clips, and a wastebasket. You could fuck in there, and no one would know the difference. Absolute privacy. Cheaper than a motel. I'll bet a lot of business executives have done it during their lunch hour. With their secretaries ending up with the imprint of scissors and paper clips on their backsides."

"I don't understand," Ostretter said, bewildered.

"On the glass-topped table," Toby explained patiently. "We didn't, of course."

"Pity," Cynthia said.

"We talked of doing it in an airliner," Toby said dreamily. "At thirty-five thousand feet. Oh darling, there's so much we've neglected. I'm dying much too soon."

"Yes, dear, you are."

"Um—ah—well..." the attorney said.

"Julie, I don't wish to be critical, but who writes your dialogue? 'Um—ah—well...' I think it needs work."

Julius Ostretter was a lawyerish lawyer: tall, deliberately solemn, cold-mannered. His speech was pedantic, though there was no denying his cleverness. If he was a lawyerish lawyer, he was also a priggish prig, the features of his coffin face pinched with self-satisfaction. He affected a round-shouldered posture, a brooding, enigmatic smile, an annoying habit of grasping his own lapels. Toby Marlow once remarked: "Julie Ostretter says 'Hello' like Abe Lincoln delivering the Second Inaugural Address."

He made a church of his fingers, tapped the tips together importantly....

"Mr. Marlow, if this inventory is accurate—and I must assume it is—you have fourteen savings accounts in banks all over the country, the sums generally between fifty and five hundred dollars. Is that assumption correct?"

Toby made a church of his fingers, tapped his tips together importantly....

"I can attest to the veracity of your statement, counselor."

"Why?" Ostretter asked.

"Why what?"

"Why do you maintain savings accounts in such places as Peoria, Illinois, and Salt Lake City, Utah—and have maintained them since the late nineteen-thirties and early nineteen-forties? Can you explain that?"

"With pleasure," Toby said. He left off mimicking the attorney and took up his dancing again. "Lawyer Ostretter, have you spoken to Jake lately?"

"Do not mention that name!" Ostretter thundered.

Toby laughed softly. "Very well. Now about the savings accounts.... In the early days of my career, when I toured the United States in various stock companies, I soon learned that most theatrical promoters and producers are direct lineal descendants of Jack the Ripper. And, having been stranded without pay and without hope of being paid in a number of cities, towns, and villages—oh God, darling, do you remember that week in Duluth?"

"Do I ever?" Cynthia exclaimed. "If it hadn't been for sex, we'd have frozen to death."

"Well, then, Lawyer Ostretter of the nameless brother, it became our habit whenever we were booked into a city or small town, to take whatever money we could spare and open an account at a local bank. In case we should ever return and be temporarily without funds—robbed again!—we would have no need to exist on peanut butter sandwiches and potato chips but could, at least, afford a bottle of Piper-Heidsieck and a train ticket to more salubrious climes."

"But some of these bankbooks go back almost forty years!"

"So? After I made it, and the movie and TV work came along, we had no need for the money. But old habits die hard, and who knows—some day I may be reduced to playing *The Drunkard* in Oshkosh, Wisconsin. Then, being hissed off the stage by those good Oshkoshians, or Oshkoshers, or Oshkoshniks, or whatever they call themselves, I could immediately repair to the local bank where I had squirreled away a goodly sum in the event of such an emergency. I still have some money in Oshkosh, don't I?"

"What? Hmm . . . Oh yes . . . here it is: more than two hundred dollars in the First Farmers Bank of Oshkosh."

"Well, there you are!" Toby said triumphantly. "Cynthia, sweet, if we ever get stranded in Oshkosh, we'll have a marvelous meal of broiled Malemute meat, or perhaps a stewed wolf."

Julius Ostretter shook his head in wonder.

"But these old accounts have increased tremendously in value. I trust you have been paying income tax on the interest earned?"

"Well—ah—the President of the United States and I have an understanding. I promised not to pay any income tax on these accounts, and he promised not to play King Lear."

"Oh my. Oh my. And I see no mention here of any life insurance policies, Mr. Marlow. Do you have any insurance at all?"

"No. None."

"A man of your means? Why, may I ask, is that?"

"What was the point of life insurance?" Toby asked. "Cynthia and I agreed quite early in our relationship that if I should die before she did, she'd have no reason to go on living. Correct, Cyn?"

"Absolutely, darling."

"Oh my, oh my, oh my. But I seem to recall a conversation we once had during which you recounted your adventures aboard a submarine with the United States Navy in World War Two. Surely you must have had service insurance?"

"Let it lapse, unfortunately, after I was honorably discharged because of wounds suffered in action. But it wasn't the Navy. I served with the U.S. Army Air Force."

"The Air Force?"

"Oh yes. Fighter pilot."

"Strange . . . I distinctly remember your telling me you were the executive officer of a submarine, and took command after the captain was incapacitated with a bad case of sunburn. You told me you sank a Japanese battleship."

"Oh no, sir." Toby laughed lightly. "I am afraid you have my military career confused with that of someone else. No, I definitely was a fighter pilot. In the European theatre. An ace, in fact. Twenty-four German fighters, twelve bombers, nine barrage balloons and, of course, locomotives, troop trains, ammunition dumps—things of that sort. But I don't like to talk about it."

"Oh . . . of course."

"How I recall those days! Waking up at dawn, wondering whether or not you were fated to see another sunrise. A quick breakfast—usually just a glass of chilled chablis and a smoked kipper. Then into your flying togs, silk scarf about your throat, and off you went into the wild blue yonder. But it all brings back too many unhappy memories—of those who didn't return. They were so young, laughing and gay. I can't talk about it."

"I under—"

"I remember once I was flying a Spitfire, and we—"

"Wasn't the Spitfire a British plane?"

"Of course. But I was testing one, you see, because they were so far superior to anything we were flying, and I had been ordered to test its flight capabilities and submit a report. A written report, directly to the White House. Well, there I was at ten thousand feet, looking for an enemy target, when suddenly I spotted a flight of three German fighters above me. I knew at once they were from Baron von Richthofen's Flying Circus. I knew that, you see, because on their wings they had this red checker-board pattern and—"

"The Red Baron's Flying Circus was in World War One."

"Of course it was! But you know how the Germans worship military tradition, and they had named one of their squadrons after the Red Baron—hero worship all down the line with those caps—and there they were, six of them, thirsting for blood. And there I was, alone and apparently a sitting duck. Well, I sized up the situation at a glance and went into an immediate power dive. Zoooommmm! And when I came down to—"

"Dear," Cynthia interrupted softly. "Weren't you supposed to meet David at the university theatre?"

"What? What? Oh yes. Well, I'm afraid we'll have to leave those Messerschmidts for another time, Julie. But remind me to tell you about the dogfight; I think you'll be interested."

"Oh I will, I will. Very interested. Now, to get back to your assets. These fifty shares of Intel-Extra. When did you buy those, Mr. Marlow?"

"Buy what?"

"Intel-Extra, Incorporated. Fifty shares of common stock. Do you recall what you paid for them?"

"Cynthia, what's that all about?"

"You remember, darling. That funny little man—the friend of Sam Beaver—was starting this company and he asked you to buy some stock and you were drunk and we wanted to help him out because he was such a *nice* little man. They send us those silly checks all the time. You cash them at the liquor store, dear."

"So I do, so I do. God takes care of fools, drunks, and actors. I think we paid a dollar a share for that stock, Lawyer Ostretter. Was that a wise investment?"

"Wise? Good gracious me! I can see you don't follow the stock reports."

"I certainly do!" Toby said indignantly. "Who they've hired, what companies are on the road, what plays they're planning. I follow the stock reports very carefully, I can tell you."

"No, no. I meant—well, let it go, Mr. Marlow. I'll have to study these documents and the inventory you've submitted. First of all, you want a will drawn. Is that correct?"

"Right."

"Now let me make a few notes here. . . . Who is to be the executor?"

"Who else but sweet Cynthia."

"Thank you, darling."

"You'll make a beautiful executor," Toby said fondly.

"Execu*trix*," the lawyer said.

"Better yet," Toby said. "Cyn knows so many wonderful tricks."

"I love you, too," she said.

"Any other beneficiaries besides your executrix?"

"Oh yes," Toby said. "A certain amount to our son, David, to our faithful retainer, Blanche, to our lovely and almost-daughter, Barbara Evings. And a few small stipends to ex-burlesque bananas currently living in abject poverty, some actors' charities, a few shekels to various friends, and memorabilia: gold cuff links, a semen-stained bedsheet from Lisbon, annotated scripts, a diary I kept for three days until the pages began to scorch, a toenail that came off after kicking an idiot who upstaged me during a performance of *Life with Father,* and several other sentimental bequests of a like nature."

Julius Ostretter sighed and began shuffling the papers and records into stacks. . . .

"Well, first let me pull all this in order and try to make some sense out of it. I will strike an approximate value to your total estate, and we can then sit down and plan specific bequests. A paid-up annuity for your wife might be best, for instance, but—"

"Oh, that's another thing," Toby said. "She's not my wife."

"Who's not your wife?" Ostretter asked.

"My wife."

"I beg your pardon?"

"Cynthia here," Toby explained. "She's not my wife. We're living in sin."

Cynthia shivered with delight.

"'Living in sin,'" she repeated. "How delicious that sounds!"

Attorney Ostretter took a deep breath.

"Perhaps I do not comprehend the situation, and if I do not, I apologize most humbly, madam. But am I to understand that you two are not legally married?"

"Good show!" Toby cried. "Now you've got it. But we've been living together for almost forty years. That gives us some points, doesn't it?"

"Forty wonderful years!" Cynthia added.

Ostretter shook his head in stupefied wonder.

"Irregular," he rumbled. "Highly irregular."

"As a matter of fact they were," Toby said cheerfully. "I'd go away for months at a time. But I always came back, didn't I, dear?"

"Always," Cynthia affirmed. "No woman could have wished for a more faithful husband."

"But I wasn't, you see," Toby said to Julius. "Not really. Her husband, I mean. In any event, now that I'm about to shuffle off to Buffalo, we thought it best,

Cynthia and I, that we be wed so that we may enjoy legally what we have for so many years enjoyed clandestinely. How did you like that speech, luv?"

"Very nice indeed," Cynthia approved. "Balanced, formal, and yet feeling, with a rolling rhythm to it."

"I rather fancied it myself," Toby said, preening. "Naturally, you are invited to the ceremony, Lawyer Ostretter—you and your charming spouse. You will, in due course, receive an official invitation, possibly engraved on the head of a pin."

"Awk!" the attorney said, disbelieving. "Awk!"

"So please make application for the proper license and necessary papers and so forth, and inform us of our duties and obligations, one of which, I understand, involves offering a libation of our royal blood to the civic authorities. Is that correct?"

"Hmm?" Ostretter said, completely rattled now. "Yes! Mm-hmm. What? Yes, oh yes! Forty years? Shocking! Must... Oh yes, *must*! Of course. Naturally. Yes, blood samples. Oh my, yes. And things . . . things to do. YOU—YOU ANIMALS!"

He screamed this last imprecation at them as he rose to his feet and rushed from the room, waving his arms wildly. He slammed the door behind him. Cynthia and Toby gazed after him in astonishment.

"Poor man," Cynthia said, shaking her head sadly. "He seemed quite upset. I wonder what on earth is bothering him?"

Toby shrugged....

"Overindulging in torts, no doubt."

SCENE TWO

ONE OF THOSE premature days in early spring: dark green buds poking, sun flexing its muscle, summer nuzzling around the edges with a warm breeze that smelled of July. The earth itself seemed to be thawing, giving up winter's heavy odor; the city stretched and sighed under a blue sky with small clouds that had been washed and hung up to dry.

Toby Marlow had insisted on hiring a victoria at the Plaza for a long ride through Central Park to David's university theatre. Cynthia had protested this extravagance, but not too vehemently; she knew the memory that inspired the decision: years ago she and Toby had intercourse, strenuously, in a London hansom. That success had resulted in what Toby called Marlow's First Law of Sexual Bliss—"Copulation without locomotion is tyranny."

Today the victoria driver was moribund, the horse feeblish; their journey was necessarily slow and wheezy. But the day was all youth and hope, the sun a glory as they wended northward on the twisty drive, surrounded by waking trees. They lolled comfortably, held hands, beamed approvingly at the beauty of this brave emerald patch set down on the steel and concrete city.

"'...So bedazzled with the sun that everything I look on seemeth green,'" Toby sighed. "And everything seemeth to be moving along in excellent fashion. We shall be married to the clarion of triumphant bells, a perfectly legal will shall be drawn, and now I may turn my full attention to making an acceptable player of our beef-witted son."

"And Barbara's problem," Cynthia reminded him. "Don't forget that. You must promise to fix that too, Toby."

"So I shall, luv, so I shall. Little Felix Fixit will put a Band-Aid on the world and make it well. But first, a small toast to the discomfiture of Lawyer Ostretter...."

He withdrew the hammered silver flask from his inside jacket pocket and proffered it to Cynthia. She shook her head, smiling. So Toby treated himself, closing his eyes in ecstasy as he swallowed.

"Ahhh!" he sighed. "'I drink no more than a sponge.' Nothing like geneva to cleanse the nasal passages of the stench of lawyers."

"Toby, why do Jacob and Julius refuse to speak to each other?"

"An argument they had, years and years ago."

"An argument? About what?"

"Neither can remember, but neither can ever forget."

"And what possessed you to tell Julie that ridiculous war story?"

"It amused me." He shrugged.

"But you're such a bad liar, Toby."

"You're wrong," he said. "I'm a very good liar."

"But it was such a silly story," she protested, "and you made so many mistakes."

"Deliberate mistakes, dear Cynthia," he said complacently. "All deliberate. Any fool can be an amateur liar and concoct a believable falsehood and tell it with a straight face. But to the professional, prevarication is a fine art—and I am a professional liar, if nothing else. What sets the professional off from the amateur is that the falsehood you relate must be intellectually unacceptable—so shot through with outrageous mistakes and exaggerations that the listener cannot possibly believe it. The lie must then succeed by its dramatic content and emotional appeal. The listener knows in his mind it's all a crock of shit, but he becomes so interested, so moved, so involved that he's willing to trust, to follow what he feels rather than what he thinks."

The dreaming horse plodded, the victoria creaked, and Cynthia puzzled over this paradox. Toby took another sip from the flask and looked about grandly, owning the world.

"Why, Toby," Cynthia said finally, "you're talking about the theatre, aren't you?"

He laughed, pressed her gloved fingertips to his lips. Then he slid an arm about her shoulders, hugged her close.

"Why in God's name couldn't David have inherited your brains as well as your looks?"

She patted his cheek lovingly.

"That's one of the nicest things you've ever said to me."

"Gin always makes me nice. Of course it's the theatre. Professional lying at its best. When that audience shows up for David's *Hamlet*, they'll be sitting on hard seats in an overheated theatre. They'll know they're not really in Elsinore, that David is not really the Prince of Denmark, that Ophelia doesn't really do a swan dive into a nearby puddle. They'll *know* those things in their minds, but they'll be willing—willing? Nay, eager!—to suppress their knowledge and swallow the lie if it interests them, moves them, involves them. That's what playing is all about—professional lying. If I could only get David to see it!"

"Do you think you could have convinced Julie Ostretter with that awful story?"

"I could," he said. "Of course I could—if you hadn't cut me short."

She looked at him coldly.

"Perhaps I cut you short because I know the true story of your war record."

"Oh God, Cyn," he groaned. "Can't you ever forgive and forget?"

"I forgave you a long time ago," she said sternly. "But no, I cannot forget. You shouldn't expect me to."

"Why the hell not?" he demanded. "You forget to tell the Chinaman not to starch my collars."

Then both were silent, sharing another memory. The spangled park disappeared. In its place appeared the squeezed, shabby kitchen of a dilapidated London flat. The year was 1941, and Britain had been under bombardment for several weeks. But age rather than bombs had crumbled this sad and seedy room.

The coin-operated gas meter was the newest

furnishing. The old table and chairs were sprung, zinc sink discolored, sagging wall shelves filled with a disheartening assortment of chipped dishes, dented pots, mismatched sets of empty jam jars. Blackout curtains hung across the narrow windows.

But despite this shoddy, the room was made bearably cheerful by what appeared to be preparations for a small celebration. The table had been spread with a reasonably clean bedsheet; an oddly assorted setting for two had been laid out. There was a loaf of greyish bread, an opened tin of meatballs and one of sardines, a box of biscuits, a jar of marmalade, a half-filled bottle of Scotch whiskey.

Cynthia, wearing the uniform of a nurse's aide, was moving about the table, inspecting her handiwork, making infinitesimal adjustments. She heard the sound of running feet pounding up the outside stairs. She started for the kitchen door. But before she reached it, it was flung back. Toby raced in, slammed the door behind him, lunged to grasp Cynthia into his arms. They exchanged passionate kisses, hugs, strokings, more kisses. . . .

"Love!" she cried. "Lover! Lover!"

"Sweet!" he cried. "Precious! Divine!"

They separated far enough to inspect each other, smiling. Toby was perfectly costumed to play the soldier returning from the wars, even though his khaki uniform was without insignia and his boots were most unmilitarily scruffy. About his shoulders hung gas mask and musette bag. And about his head was entwined a bandage, an impressive turban suitably stained.

"Oh Toby, Toby, Toby," Cynthia sighed. "How wonderful to have you home safe and sound! How long has it been?"

"Almost a week."

"Seems like two. I was so lonely and—"

Suddenly she noticed the bandage swaddling his crown. Her jaw dropped, eyes widened; she reached out timorously to touch the bandage gently.

"Oh, you poor, poor dear," she groaned. "You're wounded! Does it hurt?"

"'He jests at scars, that never felt a wound.'"

"The bombing? Oh Toby, why *didn't* you take shelter? You might have been killed!"

"Ah...well...no, not the bombing. I'll tell you later, Cyn; it's a long, long story. How are things at the hospital?"

"Dreadful," she said.

"I can imagine," he said sympathetically.

"We've been going all hours. It never lets up. I'm weary inside my bones."

"Ah-ha!" he exclaimed. "I have just the thing for inside-the-bone weariness. Take a look at this!"

He unstrapped his musette bag, carefully withdrew a bottle swathed in blue underpants. He unwrapped it with caution, then displayed it proudly to Cynthia....

"Chateau Rothschild, 1932!"

"How *nice*!" she said. "Was '32 a good year?"

"It was for me—the year I met you."

"Darling!"

She embraced him again. They kissed a very long time, and only stopped when the wail of the sirens started. They stood a moment, listening to the high-pitched warble.

"Damn, damn, damn!" he said. "The fucking alert."

"Oh, not again! I suppose we should go to the shelter?"

"The hell with it! Not before we have a glass of wine to celebrate my return from the horrors of war."

He took off his tunic, busied himself with the wine bottle and corkscrew. Cynthia sat down at the kitchen table, put chin in hand, regarded him fondly.

"How did the show go, Toby?"

"Just incredible. Max and I were *the* hit. They wouldn't let us off. What a success! It was at a big camp in Liverpool."

"I didn't know Liverpool had been bombed."

"It hasn't. But of course, we weren't *in* Liverpool. Outside, it was. Big army camp. Wonderful audience. How they laughed! We did the Flugle Street routine."

"How did you get wounded?" she asked quietly.

"Damn..." he said, "this cork is tight. If they had allowed encores, we'd have been there yet. You never heard such applause."

"How did you get hurt, Toby?"

"Here we go! Just let me try a sip. Oooh! Marvelous! Let me fill your jam jar, dear."

"Was the camp bombed?"

"Did you taste it? What flavor! What bouquet!"

"Toby, please tell me."

"Later."

"Now."

"It was sort of an accident," he said.

"A *sort* of an accident?"

"Well, if you must know, I fell out of a truck."

"I see," she said slowly. "Were you drunk?"

"Before I fell. Not after."

"Too bad you're not in the American army. You'd have gotten a Purple Heart."

"Have you heard that joke?" he inquired eagerly. "This maid in a bordello says to the madam, 'There's a soldier outside with a Purple Heart on.' And the madam says, 'I don't care what color—'"

"I heard it, Toby. What were you doing in the truck? Drunk in the truck?"

"Well, you see, after the show was such a success, some of us and some young officers went into Liverpool to celebrate. Damn it, Cyn, there's a war on! A man's got to make every minute count and grab his fun while he can."

"Oh, I agree, Toby. There *is* a war on. And who knows—your next show may be a dud. But that's a danger you must face during wartime."

"No need to get snotty about it," he said stiffly. "This was supposed to be a celebration."

"It hasn't turned out quite the way I hoped it would."

"I've been drunk before, and I'll be drunk again."

"I know, I know," she said. "It's just that I've been slaving away in that horrible hospital, seeing absolutely dreadful things, and worrying my head off about you. And now I find you've been getting drunk and falling out of trucks. Oh Toby, I don't blame you for having fun; it's just that I've had a bad week, and I'm in a vile mood. You must be extra nice and extra understanding to me tonight."

"Oh, I will, dear," he said, gulping wine. "I will indeed."

"We'll have this funny supper, and then we'll go to bed and make love, and then I'll be all right again."

"Well—ah—" he said, gulping wine. "I don't think we better do that, dear."

"But, Toby, we have all this food. It was very hard to come by. I had to beg or borrow most of it."

"No, no, it's not the supper," he said, gulping wine. "We'll definitely have the supper. Oh yes, definitely. I could eat a horse. A mare, of course. Hah!"

"We can have the supper," she said quietly, "but we can't make love. Is that what you're trying to tell me?"

"Well—ah—I don't think it would be wise."

"Why? Did you hurt something besides your head when you fell out of the truck?"

The air-raid sirens began again. And now, far off, they could hear the low, sodden crump of bombs falling.

"Second alert!" Toby said gaily. "Everyone off to the shelter!"

He smiled winningly at Cynthia, but it didn't do him a damn bit of good.

"Why can't we make love, Toby?" she asked.

"Oh...hell!" He shrugged. "It's just a precaution. Probably nothing. We'll just have to put it off for a bit, that's all."

"What have you done, Toby?"

"The shelter?" he asked hopefully.

"Toby, what have you done?"

"Well, you see, we went into Liverpool for this party. Marvelous party, really. To celebrate the success of the show, you understand. Well, then, later we went to this incredible place down near the docks. A home, really. Well, a private house. And—and..."

"And there were women there?"

"Well...yes. And whiskey, too, of course."

"Whores?"

"Oh no! No. I don't think so. Well...maybe. But very intelligent and jolly. They loved my jokes. But I really wasn't functioning too well by then, dear. The excitement and all. But it's possible they were ladies of loose virtue. Yes, that's entirely possible. And I'm not sure—I'm not completely certain—but there *is* a possibility I may have picked up something I didn't bargain for. A little extra, you might say. Nothing serious, mind you. Definitely not serious. But the doctor did say that—"

"You bastard!" she screamed. "You *bastard*!"

"Now, Cyn..."

"How dare you? How *dare* you?"

The sirens were louder now, building to an ear-piercing crescendo. And the sound of exploding bombs was louder. Anti-aircraft guns were also starting up nearby, and Toby found he needed to shout to make himself heard. Cynthia would be shouting even if the outside night were silent.

"You filthy scoundrel!" she shrieked.

She stood suddenly, upsetting her chair. She grabbed up the half-empty wine bottle from the table.

"Cynthia!" he wailed, anguised. "It was a good year!"

She hurled the wine bottle at his bandaged head. He ducked. The bottle smashed against the opposite wall; wine stained slowly downward.

"Now, Cyn..."

"Viper!"

She flung bread, tins of meatballs and sardines, jar of marmalade, whiskey bottle. Toby danced about frantically, trying to avoid the missiles.

"Now, Cyn..."

"Toad! Crawling thing!"

Toby cringed under a hail of thrown plates, pots, pans. Cynthia wrenched wooden shelves from the walls to fling them, followed by a clock, a porcelain goose in flight, and framed lithograph of Loch Lomond. All, all were hurled at the cowering Toby. The room became a shambles, and Cynthia looked about wildly for something else to throw. She leaped at the gas meter and strove mightily to wrest it from the wall, but it resisted her most strenuous efforts. Finally she desisted and stood quivering with rage, too furious to weep, too breathless to scream. Toby emerged cautiously from behind the stove.

"You're upset, aren't you?" he said.

"Upset!"

"You hate me?"

"No. Not hate you. Deceived. Betrayed."

"But I—"

"Now I know what you think of me. What you *really* think of me. Just another woman to oil your ego. I come in handy—sewing your buttons, toasting your muffins, nursing your rotten hangovers."

"There's more—"

"Don't you realize I now know what you think of

me? That I'm a lump, a post, a stupid fool of a woman who gives and gives and gives, and needs nothing in return? That's how you think of me. Admit it!"

"I swear I—"

"Toby, I exist. Can't you get that through your head? *I do exist!* I am a person, a human being, and I breathe, and think, and feel. I think things and feel things you are quite incapable of understanding, I assure you."

"When did I—"

"You think I don't know how you use me? Nurse, housekeeper, and cook. Audience for your terrible jokes, and butt of your mean and childish tricks. In that burlesque skit where you hit the other comic with a bladder—well, in our little skit, I'm the one who gets hit."

"I never—"

"I'm a woman, you brainless idiot! I'm not just a something—a something that's always there to cheat and deceive, and to hell with her. Kick her and she smiles. Hurt her and she holds out loving arms."

"But I—"

"And another thing . . . If I ever—"

"Goddammit!" he screamed. "Will you never let me finish a sentence?"

"You just did," she said coldly. "If I ever—"

Again she halted. They both looked instinctively upward. They heard the scream of falling bombs, muffled explosions, the wail of fire engines. Their house was shaken; somewhere glass shattered and tinkled down to the street.

"If I ever did love you—" Cynthia went on, "for what reason I no longer know—you have succeeded in killing that love. Poor, tender little thing. It might have taken root and bloomed, but you put your great, cruel heel on it and ground it and ground it until it was nothing, *is* nothing. I hope you're proud of that."

They were silent then, glaring at each other, oblivious to the pandemonium in the city around them. Finally . . .

"Are you finished?" Toby asked.

"Yes."

"*Quite* finished?"

"Yes. Oh no—just one more thing. You're a shithead. Now I'm finished."

"You always were a lousy player," he said. "That could have been a great scene, and you muffed it."

"I wasn't playing," Cynthia said with grand dignity.

"You were speaking from the heart?"

"I was," she said.

"Too bad you lack the training and experience to be sincere. Look, Cynthia, I admit I am not the easiest man in the world to live with."

"Hah!"

"I admit I lie, cheat, and even, on occasion, steal. I admit I deceive you and betray you."

"Hah!"

"I admit I take advantage of your sweet good nature, and that, infrequently, I have not given proper consideration to your needs and wishes and hopes."

"Hah!"

"But I *am* capable of forgiving a woman who shouts 'Hah!' to everything I say. I forgive you a great many things, Cynthia, most of which you probably are not aware of. But I don't think of it as forgiving because I love you, for who you are and what you are. I know you are not a lump, a post, a foolish woman. And I know I am egotistical, self-centered, and rarely do anything I don't want to do. But have I ever denied what I am? Have I ever tried to conceal from you my true nature? You know I haven't."

"But you never—"

"No, now stop. You did your turn; I'm on now. I've always shown myself to you with all my warts, pimples, scars, and bald head. No makeup. I've hidden nothing from you. And I've always assumed that if you didn't like what you saw, you had the intelligence and courage to walk away from me. But you've stayed."

"I've stayed because I thought I could change you."

"I never want to change *you*."

There was a pause....

"Thank you," she said faintly.

There was a heavy crump of exploding bombs, closer now. The lights flickered wildly. They heard the wail of sirens, shouts in the street, the continuous barking of anti-aircraft guns....

"Cynthia," Toby said tenderly, "you're deluding yourself if you think you want me different from what I am. In your heart of hearts, you're content with what I am—or at least with the image you have of me. Occasionally, only occasionally, you are so horrified by what I do that you cry, 'Why can't Toby be like other men?' But you know, don't you, Cyn, that if I was like other men, I'd feel very differently about you, and you about me. We make a marvelous cast, you and I, the way we are. Let's stick to our parts and not try to rewrite the lines. Our life together *plays*, darling. I feel it, and I think you feel it, too. Don't you?"

No answer.

"Don't you feel it, Cyn?"

"Yes," she sighed. "It's just..."

"I know, I know," he said. "I've been a bastard. Again. And you were disappointed in me. Again. That's why you said those silly things and threw stuff and tore up the place."

"I suppose."

"Oh darling, darling..."

He moved to her swiftly and embraced her, clasping her waist, stroking her hair. Finally, finally, she relaxed into his arms, hugged him fiercely.

"Cynthia, promise me you'll never again attack me in that vulgar and primitive fashion."

"I promise, Toby."

"Promise you'll never, as long as you live, throw another dinner plate, soup kettle, or salt shaker at me."

"I promise. Oh, I promise, dear!"

They were embracing again when a stick of bombs fell across their square of flats. There was a tremendous crash. The lights flickered, went off, came back on again to show the ceiling had fallen, the outside wall had been blown away to reveal London burning. The air was filled with smoke and plaster dust.

Cynthia and Toby had been knocked off their feet. They crawled shakily from under the rubble, staggered upright. They brushed debris and plaster chunks from their heads and clothes.

"Goddammit, Cyn." Toby coughed. "You *promised*!"

But now the sun was shining, Central Park was greening. It was another world, another spring. They listened to the clop of the horse's hooves, creak of the victoria's wheels. Cynthia and Toby were carried in a new dream up to the university theatre. Toby took out his flask again, held it up so it glinted flashing in the sunlight.

"To wedded bliss!" he toasted.

"I must drink to that!" Cynthia said.

They each took a sip from the flask. Then Toby returned it to his pocket and resumed his former position, his arm about Cynthia's shoulders.

"Glad we're getting married, Cyn?"

"We've always been married."

"I know," he said. "But now you'll have a piece of paper signed by the Commissioner of Sanitation—or *someone*. As for me, I'm all choked up and giggly and nervous. You *will* be kind to me on our wedding night, won't you?"

"I'll be ever so gentle and understanding."

"I can see it now," Toby said dreamily. "After the sumptuous wedding feast, we shall be blessed by the assembled company and then, in a rain of flowers, we shall retire to the nuptial chamber. And then you will coyly excuse yourself to go into the dressing room and change into a negligee."

"And you'll be right in there with me."

"Of course," he agreed. "I must buy you a special negligee for the wedding night. Something in black lace with pink ribbons and a badge that says 'Garter Inspector.' As for myself, I intend to wear a new pair of tweed pajamas with the pins still in them, cuffs over my knuckles, and a drawstring that goes around me three times. Oh Cyn, we're going to be so happy together!"

Suddenly she broke and began weeping. She turned to bury her face against his chest, clutching him to her.

"What's this, what's this?" he said. "Come on, darling. What happened to all your brave promises? No tears and no regrets. Remember? That's what we agreed."

"I lied," she sobbed. "I lied!"

"No fair. That's my line."

"I don't want to live without you," she said dully.

"Very understandable, luv; I don't want to live without me either. But I'm hanging on. You can, too. You've never failed me yet. Don't start now."

She straightened, sniffed, took a tissue from her bag and dabbed at her eyes.

"I'm sorry, Toby," she said, biting her lower lip.

"You plenty woman," he said tenderly. "You cook good, give me man-child, keep house, work hard, smell nice. I tell chief; he give me you. You be my number-one wife."

"I've never been unfaithful to you, Toby. Never! In my whole life."

"I know you haven't, baby. And it was a dirty trick. Just to make me feel guiltier."

"I didn't mind. Truly I didn't. As long as you came back."

"Why do you endure me, Cyn?"

"Because you're the only man who makes me feel alive. I'm dead without you, Toby. Oh, I might breathe and move around and talk and smile. But inside I'm just dead and nothing counts. Without you...

He embraced her.

"Beautiful, beautiful words, darling. Will couldn't have said it half as well. Cyn..."

"Yes, Toby?"

"Our wedding night. In bed together. I want it to be something special."

"I do too, dear."

"Do you think you could manage to get the hiccups?"

SCENE THREE

AT FIRST GLANCE the stage of the university theatre appeared bare, empty, unset. A brick wall was at the rear. Above, the fly was cluttered with dead lights, hoists, pulleys, sandbags, a catwalk, etc. The wings were a jumble of scenery flats: sections of a stone fence, library paneling, a false door that would never open, painted fireplace, a net of foliage, etc.

But on closer examination, it became evident this empty stage was actually set; the setting was that of a bare stage. That brick wall in the rear was a canvas drop. The overhead lights, catwalk, scenery flats in the wings—all dummies, artfully designed and arranged to give the illusion of a vacant stage.

There was not much on the apron, but a few props enhanced the impression of an undecorated stage being used for early rehearsals. There was a rickety kitchen table, four plain wooden chairs. Upstage, beyond the proscenium arch, was a rough wooden box, actually a large packing crate. This was plainly labeled "Property of Costume Department." It was filled with a variety of hats.

The only illumination in this hollow and echoing place came from a single electric bulb fastened atop an eye-level pipe extending from a metal base.

David Marlow was seated at the kitchen table. He was wearing a dark, vested business suit. Heavy eyeglasses in place, he was studying a playscript. His father was bent over the crate of hats in the rear, rummaging...

"Where's Mother?" David asked, not looking up from his script. "I thought she was coming with you."

Toby Marlow straightened up, faced the missing audience. He was wearing the cocked hat of an eighteenth-century admiral. He stalked forward majestically and, in pompous bearing and rolling gait, he *was* an admiral. He slowly raised a nonexistent telescope to his eye, slowly scanned a nonexistent horizon for a nonexistent enemy.

"She took the carriage back to Saks," he said. "She wants to buy favors for the wedding."

Still paying no attention to his father's antics, David said absently, "I suppose she's all excited and fluttery about getting married."

"Let me tell you something about your mother, m'lad. She's been playing Spring Byington all her life, but deep down inside she's Norma Shearer, and don't you ever forget it. Where's Barbara?"

"She'll be along later," David said. "Right now she's over at the Fine Arts Center doing those silly little drawings of hers."

Toby had exchanged the admiral's hat for the high, hard bowler of a Victorian detective or thug. Now his hunched walk was menacing, his manner brutal.

"Well, let's get at your silly little performance. Three more weeks and you'll be exhibiting your ineptitude to the world."

"I know," David said "I know. You don't have to remind me."

"Butterflies, kiddo?" Toby jeered. "Sweat beginning to crawl down the spine? A weakness in the knees and a looseness in the bowels? The lines disappearing from your memory overnight and a wild desire to take a rocket to the moon?"

David looked up then and glared at his father.

"Just shut up, will you?" he said fiercely. "I'll be all right."

"The hell you will—unless you show me more than you have so far. How did the rehearsal go?"

"Not so good. I've got to come back tonight. Just Watkins—he's the director—and me. I think he's worried."

"Worried? If I was him I'd be hysterical, and you'd be out on your ass. All right, what do you want to do?"

David rose and held the playscript out to Toby....

"'Oh that this too too solid flesh...'"

Toby waved the book away.

"I don't need it. I knew that speech before I knew 'There was a young man from Racine...' All right, let's hear it. Take it from the top."

"'Oh that—'"

"Stop," Toby said immediately. "Do me a favor, will you? Take off those cheaters. Playing Hamlet in hornrims is like making love in hip boots."

David removed the glasses. He stood in front of the table, facing upstage. Toby wandered about behind him, rummaging again through the crate of hats.

"'Oh that this too too solid flesh would—'"

"Stop," Toby said again. "Look at your script. That first word. It's not 'Oh'—O-h; it's the single capital letter 'O' followed by an exclamation point. Right?"

David flipped through pages of the script, looking for the speech.

"Well . . . yes," he said finally. "But what difference does it make?"

Toby came out of the crate wearing a cardinal's biretta. He moved upstage with great, slow dignity, a soft, forgiving smile on his face. He swept imaginary robes about him and made the sign of the Cross in an elegant blessing over all the empty seats in the darkened theatre.

"No difference at all," he told David. "Just whether the lady comes or doesn't come. Will you listen to me, for God's sake? Hamlet is making a cry of despair. So Will has him shout 'O!' Single letter 'O' followed by exclamation point. Will knew what he was doing—which is more than I can say for you, Count Dreckela. You give this cry as 'Oh'—O-h. Now listen to the difference. 'O!' Hear how short and full of pain that single letter is? It's Hamlet's despair, coming right out of his gonads. Now here's the way you do it: 'Oh.' You're getting that o-h sound in there. It's like you said, 'Ohhh!' You're drawing it out and making it soft, like a constipated moan. But it's a fucking cry, a sharp cry of pain. 'O!' Can't you hear it? One letter, one syllable, one emotion that tears your goddamn heart out. Try it again."

"'O!'" David cried.

"Well . . ." Toby sighed. "Where there's an oi, there's a vay. It's better. Lousy, but better. All right, start again."

"'O! that this too too solid—'"

"Stop again. Tutu? What the hell are you talking about—ballet skirts? It's two separate words: too and too. 'O! that this *too too* solid flesh would melt . . .' Will didn't use just a single 'too,' he used a couple of them. Trust his instinct. And enunciate, for Chrissake. The peasants in the balcony want to hear you. They paid less for their tickets, but it means more to them. Play to the peanut gallery, you creep! Take it again."

"'O! that this too too solid flesh would melt, thaw and resolve itself into a dew; or that the Everlasting—'"

"Stop," Toby said. "Please stop," he pleaded. "Stop, stop, stop! I can't bear to hear the mighty Will scorned and brought so low."

Now Toby was wearing a cowboy's sombrero, strutting with exaggeratedly bowed legs. His hands hovered near imaginary guns. He took a few steps away from David, than whirled suddenly, his face contorted and mean. Thumbs in the air, his extended forefingers jerked at David.

"Pow!" Toby shouted. "Pow! Pow! Pow! Look, sonny, you want a pause after the word 'dew.' Hamlet wants his body dissolved; he doesn't want to exist. Then he gets another idea; he could commit suicide if God had not said that suicide is a no-no. But it takes him a moment to get this idea. He's thinking all the time, you see. Even while he's talking. So you pause a bit. Take a beat of one or two, and then you deliver this new idea. Try it again."

"'O! that this too too solid flesh would melt, thaw and resolve itself into a dew . . . Or that the Everlasting had not fixed his canon 'gainst self-slaughter. O God! O God! How weary, stale, flat and unprofitable seem to me all the uses of this world.'"

Toby Marlow was silent a moment, staring at his son. Then he sighed deeply.

"Did you ever consider pimping or basket-weaving as a career?" he inquired. "Look, you're coming up on that final line when you should be going down. It's not a cry of exultation, for God's sake! Hamlet's already said he wants his flesh to melt. But he knows that isn't possible. And he can't slit his own throat because God says that's naughty. So the final line is a summing-up: a dull, sad realization that he can't win. 'How weary, stale, flat and unprofitable seem to me all the uses of this world.' You make it sound like The Battle Cry of Freedom! Can't you understand what Hamlet is saying, thou lily-liver'd boy? Suddenly Hamlet is old. He's an old, old man, long before his time. He's lived too much. Nothing has flavor any more. Nothing has meaning. That line is a lament, the lament of an old man."

"You should know," David said furiously. "How to grow old disgracefully—you're an expert at that!"

"Old?" Toby shouted. "Yes, goddamn it, I'm old. And shall I tell you what it's like? The cock shrinks and the ass sinks. You wake up in the morning belching and farting. Your breath is a terror and all you can remember is childhood. You dream more than you do. And then, one day, little animals get in your gut and eat you up. But of course you'll never know all that. You'll be young forever. Peter Pan! Hello, Peter Pan!"

"You go to hell!" David screamed.

"I did," Toby said. "Years ago. It's something like Yonkers."

They were silent then, glaring at each other, quivering with their fury. Toby turned away first. He went back to the costume crate, dug out a high silk topper. He walked about the dusty stage with belly thrust out, a bloated capitalist. He doffed his fine hat right and left to the admiring multitudes.

"All right," he said finally, "take it from the top."

"Again?" David asked despairingly.

"Yes, again, you—you *mechanic*! And try to give it something this time."

"'O! that this too too solid flesh would melt, thaw and resolve itself into a dew. Or that the Everlasting had not fix'd his canon 'gainst self-slaughter. O God! O

God! How weary, stale, flat and unprofitable seem to me all the uses of this world.'"

David turned to look at his father, awaiting his judgment. Toby paced back and forth, top hat pushed to the back of his head. He took out his flask, helped himself to a deep swallow while continuing to pace.

"Not bad," he muttered. "Not bad."

"I thought you said I was lousy."

"I changed my mind."

"It's got to be an improvement!"

"I didn't say you were good," Toby said. "Just not bad. Not *too* bad. There's something there. Something. But it's not coming through. Block. There's a block there. Listen, Mandrake the Magician, what do you think about when you deliver that speech? What's your motivation? Come on, don't be ashamed. You can tell your dear old daddy."

"Well," David said, putting on his glasses, "as you—"

"Take off those damned specs!" Toby roared. "Don't hide from me, thou jelly-eyed knave!"

David compromised; he shoved the glasses atop his head.

"As you said, that speech is a lament. I think of how difficult it is to live—just to live! All the things that go wrong... It's hard enough just to exist and earn a living, but life closes in. You and Mother aren't married, so I'm a bastard. I've knocked up Barbara, and she won't marry me. You're dying, and there's nothing I can do about it. I've got this great chance, but I'm insecure. All that's my motivation."

"Gee," Toby said, "that's swell."

He went back to the box of hats, selected a guardsman's busby. Stiffly erect, swinging his arms in the British fashion, he began a kind of military drill. He paced up and down, stamped his foot, did a sharp about-face, etc.

"Got it all cut down to size, haven't you?" he sneered. "*Your* size. Hamlet happens to be a prince of Denmark. A *prince*! And his father was the king. A *king*! And his mother has married his murdering uncle in 'most unseemly haste.' But all this—having to do with big people of dignity and importance and outsize passions—you reduce to your bastardy and your piddling little ambitions and the fact that the woman you've inflated with your reckless gism is now—"

"Oh my God, can you never understand? I have nothing to do with princes and kings of Denmark who lived a thousand years ago. I've got to have motives I can understand and feel. I am *not* Hamlet; I am *not* the Prince of Denmark. I am *me*. And all I can express is what I am. Don't expect any more of me than that. I will not *play* at acting. I will not assume emotions I do not feel. I do not want to be Hamlet or Captain Brassbound or the Great White Hope. If I'm going to be anything at all, I must be *myself*, what I am and what I feel. Everything else is faking."

"You think I'm a faker?" Toby demanded.

"Yes!" David said, nodding wildly. "Yes! You're a faker. A con man. A pretender. A player!"

His father stared at him.

"If you had a brain," he said, "you'd be dangerous."

Barbara Evings entered, drifting in quietly from the wings. She was wearing something earth-colored and flowing. She heard the last shouted exchange, but neither man noticed her. She floated down onto the dusty stage, sitting silently, watching father and son intently.

"A faker, eh?" Toby said. "Well, I've already told you what you are—so enamored of your own ego that you can't communicate, onstage or off. You just can't open up. There's no passion in you."

"You're referring to that conversation we had along the park, I presume?"

"'I presume, I presume,'" Toby mimicked. "You're beginning to talk like a ruptured bookkeeper. Yes, you presume correctly."

"Well, I've been thinking—"

"I thought I smelled rubber burning."

"Ho ho, Dad, that's rich. I've been thinking about your ridiculous claim that we all play roles constantly, not only onstage but in our relations with other people. And that an individual is nothing but the sum of the parts he plays."

"Well . . . yes," Toby said warily. "That's about what I said."

"Don't weasel, you weasel," David said scornfully. "That's *exactly* what you said. And what you believe?"

"Yes."

"You're sure of that?"

"Who the hell are you playing now—Perry Mason? I'm not on trial, for God's sake."

"I just want to make sure I've understood you."

Toby donned a beret, cocked it over one eye. He shoved hands into pockets, hunched his shoulders, pouted his lower lip. He slouched about the stage, creating a Parisian Apache.

"Merde!" he rasped. "Get on with it, espece de dingue!"

"If you believe all that," David said triumphantly, "then how do you account for the fact that good actors—I mean the great ones, the stars—how do you account for the fact that they project their own personalities no matter what roles they play?"

"What?" Toby said, confused. "What? I don't follow you."

"The hell you don't." David cried delightedly. "You're demolished and stalling for time to think of an answer. You yourself have told me a dozen times that Hampden was Hampden no matter what part he played. And so, reportedly, was Henry Irving. And so was Barrymore. And so is Olivier and Richardson and Gielgud. No matter what parts they played—king or commoner, lover or clown—the essential personality of the man comes through. His performance in a role is unique, different from the performance of another great actor in the same part."

"So? So?" Toby demanded, agitated now. "What's the point? What are you saying?"

"You know damned well what I'm saying. That actors, great actors, are not merely players. They are artists. They bring something extra to their work— their ego or soul or whatever the hell you want to call it. But the fact that this very personal quality they have comes through—no matter what the makeup or costume or lines they speak—this proves there is an essence, a unique essence, that goes beyond merely 'playing a part' and triumphs over it. That's why you're not a great actor and never have been. That's why no one ever wanted you to do Hamlet. Because you are what you said—merely the sum of the parts you've played. You've never made that final step to greatness because you have no unique essence. You don't know who you are."

Toby was plainly rattled. He tossed the beret back into the crate, fumbled about for a new hat, then turned away. He uncapped his flask again and took a deep swallow, then left the opened flask on the kitchen table.

David defiantly slid his glasses into place and stared owl-eyed at his father.

"Well?" he asked. "What have you to say to that?"

"If I had my wits about me, I'd iambic you to death or annihilate you with a trochee."

"If you had your usual half-measure of wits about you, you'd admit the truth of what I just said, that—"

"I admit nothing!" Toby thundered. "I am not now

nor have I ever been a member of the wrinkled-assed school of acting."

"That there is a unique essence in each of us," David went on inexorably, "that good actors express creatively on the stage. And, with enough talent and the right technique—no tricks!—that ego is revealed as something splendid and moving. A piece of the truth. When I look for my motivation, Toby, I'm just trying to discover who I am, *what* I am. It's not easy. Sometimes it's painful. But it's what I want to do. I want to be a great actor. I want to create on the stage the same moments of truth you know when you look at an El Greco or read Shelley or hear Bach. What's so awful about that?"

Toby went over to his son and unexpectedly stroked his head. His hand remained on the back of David's hair.

"My sweet, sweet bastard," Toby said tenderly. "I love you. Do you know that?"

David couldn't raise his eyes, couldn't look at him.

"Yes," he said in a low voice. "I know."

"Good. And I'm going to make a great player—all right, all right, a great *actor*—out of you before I die."

"I have to do it my own way."

"There's nothing wrong with you that time and an enema won't cure. Can't we keep working together?"

"Of course," David said.

"Keep on the lines. If nothing else, speak in a loud, clear voice. Speak to the balcony and beyond."

"Beyond?"

"God deserves a good laugh."

"Go fuck yourself," David said.

"Don't think I haven't tried," Toby said. He turned away to leave. He saw Barbara Evings curled up on the stage. He went over to her. "Ahh, Rima, the Cat Girl. How long have you been there?"

"Not very long," Barbara said. "You were arguing when I came in, but then you ended up loving."

"Yes," Toby said, touching her cheek. "We ended up loving. That's the way to end up, baby. Would you like to come home and tickle me off with feathers?"

"If you want me to, Toby. I love feathers."

He laughed and started to stoop, to kiss her. But his features wrenched with pain, he clapped a hand to his ribs. He stood bent over a moment, eyes closed, waiting for the spasm to pass. Then he straightened slowly, smiled wanly at Barbara.

"Something that ate me," he said. "Ta-ta, luv."

He flipped a hand casually at David and walked off the stage steadily.

David had been silent and brooding during this exchange. After Toby departed, David saw the flask on the table. He made a movement toward the wings, to call Toby back. Then he checked himself and picked up the flask.

"I think I'll have a small drink," he said loudly. "I'm beginning to like it."

"I know," Barbara said.

"Would you like a sip?"

"No, thank you."

"Well, get off the floor and come sit over here. You'll catch a cold in your ass."

Barbara rose awkwardly and moved over to the table. She lowered herself into one of the plain wooden chairs. David took off his glasses, rubbed his eyes wearily. He started to replace his spectacles, then folded them and slid them into his jacket pocket. He stood up, began to pace about the stage, mostly behind Barbara. His head was down. He stared at the bare boards.

"Oh wow," he said. "What a session that was! You wouldn't believe the screaming."

"But you ended friends?"

"Of course. But..."

"But what?"

"Bobbie, his ideas are so old-fashioned, so out-of-date. The old fart!"

"But you love him, David?"

"Oh sure. The monster! He knows so much."

"About what?"

"The stage. Theatre. Tricks. Lighting. Makeup. Audiences. All the techniques. Fantasy. He's always on, you know. The curtain went up when he was born, and it's never come down... yet."

"He's always performing? Is that what you mean?"

"Oh yes. Lights in his face, embracing the audience, bellowing to the gallery. But I don't know who he is. And he doesn't either."

In his wanderings, David came abreast of the wooden crate. He stopped and turned over a few of the hats. He selected a steel helmet of World War I vintage, a doughboy's helmet. He strapped it on. Crouching, he began to search about warily, grasping an imaginary rifle, a soldier on patrol.

"David, he's *Toby*."

"Who is Toby Marlow?" David demanded. "He's played a million parts. He knows five languages, ten accents, twenty dialects. Better than any actor I've ever heard. His philosophy is a stew of playwrights' ideas, and his conversation is bits and pieces of other men's words. But who the hell is *he*?"

David traded the helmet for a fez and began to do a greasy headwaiter or Cairo guide, bowing and scraping, a horribly oily smile on his face.

"David, Toby is your *father*."

"Oh, yes," David said gloomily. "My unmarried father. And I'm his 'sweet, sweet bastard.' What hurts is that he gets to me, he *gets* to me! He's such a player. He can make me laugh and he can make me cry. Against my will, mind you. But I don't know where the greasepaint ends and he begins. Can't you understand? I don't know who he *is*."

"Is it important?"

"Of course it's important. I don't want my father to be a clown in a fright wig and a painted mask."

"Aren't we all?" she said.

"What the hell is that supposed to mean?"

"I don't know." She shrugged. "It seemed very profound to me, so I said it."

"Well, it's not profound."

"Yes, David."

He tossed the fez back into the crate and came over to the table where Barbara was sitting. He pulled up a chair and sat down across from her, leaning forward onto the table.

"He's still a burlesque banana," he grumbled. "With a putty nose. Hitting people with bladders and making dirty jokes. He's *playing* at living."

"Yes, David."

"Will you please stop saying, 'Yes, David'? I will not be patted on the head and humored."

"Yes, David."

"One last time—will you marry me?"

"One last time—no."

He stared at her, drew a deep breath.

"Why not?" he asked.

"You're not Toby," she said.

He tried to laugh.

"Sorry. My mother got there first. He's going to marry her."

"You know that's not what I meant."

"I know what you meant—that I'm not the man my father is."

"Yes," she said determinedly. "That's what I meant. You're not the man your father is."

"I thank you very much."

He tilted back his head, took a long swig from the flask. He coughed, spluttered, wiped the back of his hand across his eyes. Then he took a deep breath. He wouldn't look at her.

"Now you're angry with me, aren't you?" she said.

"You, Toby, myself," he said. "I don't know who. Or what. Oh God, Barbara, what *am* I going to do?"

"Are you frightened?"

"No. Yes. I don't know."

"Frightened about playing Hamlet?"

"*Acting* Hamlet. That, and you, and Toby dying. Suddenly I'm not sure. Suddenly I realize I can't control things. My confidence is just *oozing* away. What a sensation! Like watching your blood flow out, and you can't stop it."

"You were confident enough the night we met. You were so sure of yourself, so sure."

"That night!" he cried. "If I could only feel again what I felt that night!"

"As I recall," she said, "you felt me."

He laughed ruefully.

"You—amongst other things . . ."

They both smiled gently, remembering . . . They stared at the bare electric bulb atop the pipe stand. It began to grow in size—a grapefruit, a melon, a pumpkin. It became huge, softly luminous, and floated up higher, higher, into the darkness. Then it was a full moon, plump and juicy, hanging over a splashing sea. The Cape Cod beach was etched into white dunes, black shadows.

The year was 1973. Toby Marlow was playing summer stock in Provincetown, and David had come up from Manhattan to catch his father in *The Man Who Came to Dinner*. Toby had been at his outrageous best: snarling, hacking, wind-milling, belching, "catching flies," and interpolating whispered asides that would have enraged the playwrights, but convulsed the audience.

At midnight, leaving his father to the sickening adulation of the dressing-room mob, David Marlow went strolling slowly along the shore. He breathed deeply, surrendering to the seductive night. He looked up at the sky dreamily, eyeglasses glittering. His hands were clasped behind him as he paced, and quoted ...

"'How sweet the moonlight sleeps upon this bank! Here will we sit and let the sounds of music creep in our ears: soft stillness and—'"

But suddenly his recital was interrupted by a series of loud female screams coming from seaward. David halted, trembled, stared fearfully.

"My God!" he said aloud.

The screams concluded with a trill, then changed to words:

"Au secours! Au secours! Aidez-moi! Aidez-moi!"

David giggled nervously. "She's either French or a fearful snob."

He whipped off his glasses, set them carefully aside in the sand. He backed off two steps, set himself—and after a moment's hesitation (only a moment) dashed bravely into the mild surf. He paused when the sea reached his knees.

"Halloo?" he yelled. "Halloo?"

"Halloo!" the call came back. "Halloo!"

David turned toward the voice, waded out farther until the water was lapping at his thighs. He looked about frantically.

"Halloo? Halloo?"

"Halloo! Halloo!"

Manfully he struggled out deeper. The ocean was up to his waist now. He realized it had filled his pockets: his trousers were beginning to droop.

"Halloo?" he screamed desperately.

"Halloo!"

"Where are you?" he shouted.

"Here! I'm here!"

"Where the goddamn hell is *here*?"

There was a short pause. Then a feminine voice said firmly, "There is no need for profanity."

A slim white arm came out of the sea, just a few yards beyond David. He strove forward mightily, waves up to his chest now. He leaned ahead to grasp a hand, a wrist, an arm.

"All right," he said loudly. "Don't fight me. You're safe now. I have you."

"I have no clothes on."

"Shall I turn my back?" he asked bitterly.

Without waiting for an answer, he swooped, picked up the young woman in his arms, began staggering back toward shore. She tilted her head back over his arm, stared upward.

"Courage." he gasped. "Just a little further now."

"What a glorious night!" she said. "Have you ever seen such stars?"

He regained the beach, breathing heavily. The sea streamed from his sodden clothes. He stumbled up onto dry sand. Then he stood, chest heaving, suddenly conscious that he was holding something that felt like a peeled snake.

"You may put me down now, thank you," she said.

"Shouldn't I do something?" he asked.

"Like what?"

"Well ... like roll you over a barrel?"

"Do you have a barrel?"

"Unfortunately not."

"Well then?"

"How about mouth-to-mouth resuscitation?"

"No, thank you," she said stiffly. "I don't wish to become involved. *Will* you put me down, please?"

"I would, but I left my eyeglasses in the sand

somewhere, and I don't want you stepping on them."

"Well, look for them."

"Yes. All right."

Still carrying her, he shuffled damply down the beach a few steps, both of them searching the sand.

"No," he said, "this doesn't look familiar. Must be the other way."

He turned around, the dripping burden in his arms gaining weight every moment. He lurched in the opposite direction, hearing himself slosh.

"What do your glasses look like?" she asked.

"Well—you know—glasses. Black horn-rims. Rather handsome, actually. You can't miss them."

"There!" she said. "Over there. Toward the water."

"No, that's a beer can. Oh . . . there they are."

He carried her a bit farther inland, across the beach. He was bent almost double, panting and wheezing with his exertions. Her wet flesh was slowly slipping from his grasp.

"I'm going to set you down now," he said. "Please don't step on the glasses."

"I won't."

Carefully, with a final effort, he set her slowly down on her feet. Then he straightened up with a sigh of relief. But he had released her too soon; her knees buckled, she sat suddenly on the sand.

"My God!" he groaned, anguished. "You sat on my glasses!"

"I didn't."

"You did, you did! You sat down on top of them."

She rolled sideways onto one hip. She explored the sand beneath her. She came up with the glasses, examined them, blew sand away. Then she handed them up to David.

"There you are," she said. "Good as new."

David put them on immediately, stared up at the moon.

"Loose," he said angrily. "The right earpiece is definitely loose."

"I'm sorry," she said in a small voice.

He stared down at her, took an involuntary step backward.

"My God," he gasped, "you're naked!"

"I told you I was."

"I know, but I didn't think you'd be so—so *bare*. Is that an appendicitis scar?"

"Yes."

"It's charming."

"Thank you. Might I borrow your jacket? The wind is chilly."

"Oh . . . of course. I should have thought of that. It's soaked, I'm afraid."

"That's all right. So am I."

David peeled off his wet jacket. He tried to squeeze out excess moisture, then flapped it a few times in the breeze. He draped it tenderly about her shoulders, helping her to turn up the collar, tuck the tails in snugly. Then he sat down on the sand alongside her, hugging his drawn-up knees.

"Where are your clothes?" he asked her.

"I took them off."

"Oh? Were they dragging you down?"

"Oh no," she said. "They're down the beach somewhere. I was committing suicide, and I wanted to be naked. Just as I came into the world."

He was so horrified, so pained by what she said that he wanted to weep.

"Suicide? My God! But if—if—"

"If I was committing suicide, why did I cry out?"

"Yes," he nodded. "Why did you?"

"I changed my mind."

"I see."

She turned to stare at him.

"Do you? Do you really?"

"Not really," he confessed. "My name is David Marlow."

"Mine is Barbara Evings," she said. "I'm very glad to meet you. I suppose if you hadn't come along, I'd be dead this very minute."

"I suppose so," he agreed. "I was going straight home tonight—I have some very important reading to do—but then I decided to take a walk along the shore; the night is so beautiful. I was going to walk only a few minutes and go home. But then I heard you scream. It's all chance, isn't it?"

"What is?"

"Well, I mean my suddenly deciding to walk along the shore, and your deciding that you didn't want to drown. All chance."

"Well . . . yes," she said doubtfully. "Unless . . ."

"Unless what?"

"Nothing. Really nothing . . ."

They were silent then, sitting with shoulders touching in identical positions: knees bent and clasped. Now they carefully avoided looking at each other. They carefully inspected the moon, stars, scudding clouds. It was all there—but it was beginning to tilt.

"Why did you shout in French?" he asked curiously.

"I'm studying it," she told him. "It's a lovely language, but I have trouble with the genders."

"Everyone does," he assured her. "Especially the French. If it's not too painful to discuss, could you tell me why you wanted to kill yourself?"

"Because I decided that life has no value."

"And why did you decide *not* to kill yourself?"

"Because, when I was going down for the fourth time, I realized that if life has no value, then suicide is meaningless."

Then he looked at her. Admiringly.

"You're very deep," he said.

"I almost was," she said.

"What? Oh yes! But why do you feel life has no value?"

She squirmed on the sand, turning to face him. She thrust her head forward until their noses were quite close. She stared intently into his eyes.

"Do you know how many people in this world die of starvation every day?" she demanded.

It was almost an accusation; he felt uneasy.

"Not exactly," he said. "Hundreds, I suppose."

"Thousands!" she assured him. "And I'm sure you read about that earthquake in Tibet?"

"Oh yes. I read about it. Terrible."

"Horrible," she nodded. "And off the coast of Peru, all the anchovies are dying."

"Is that why you feel life has no value?"

"Yes. But then I discovered death doesn't either. There's really *nothing* for us, is there?"

"You mustn't feel that way," he said earnestly. "People have things."

"Ho!" she said. "What do you have?"

"Ambition. Dreams."

"About what?"

"Being a great actor. Some day . . ."

She turned her head sideways, laid her cheek on her clasped knees. He couldn't see her eyes, but he was certain they were sad and defeated.

"I don't have any ambition," she said in a low voice. "Or dreams about anything. I'm just empty."

"Barbara, don't say that!"

"It's true, David. I have absolutely no future. None at all. And my past has been rather uneventful, too. Would you believe that the most exciting thing that's ever happened to me was winning a contest where you had to guess how many aspirins were in a big jar in a druggist's window?"

"What did you win?"

"The aspirins," she said. "That's not very exciting, is it?"

"No," he admitted, "not very. But my God, you've got so much going for you! You're a beautiful woman."

"I'm not," she said, lifting her chin, wetting her lips with her tongue. "I'm not beautiful."

"You are, you really are. Your hair is gorgeous."

"Oh this old thing," she said, trying to comb out tangles with her fingers. "It's all wet and matted and smells of carp."

He leaned to her, thrust his nose into the tangles, inhaled deeply.

"Not carp," he breathed. "It smells of the salt sea. Wild. And you have great eyes."

She rolled them to the moon.

"They're too close together," she said.

"No, no!" he protested. "Just the right distance. Also, your mouth is lovely."

She pouted slightly, and made little guppy movements.

"Aren't my lips too thin?" she said.

"I should say not! Your lips are full and beautifully shaped."

She lifted her head, turned it slowly back and forth.

"My neck is too long?" she suggested.

"Absolutely not!" he said firmly. "Slender and swanlike. Definitely swanlike."

She looked down at herself sorrowfully.

"I have no breasts," she said.

"You do, too! Elegant and exciting."

"Elegant?"

"Really."

"Exciting?"

"Scout's honor."

But then she shook her head dolefully.

"My hips are too wide," she said.

"How can you say that?" he demanded. "Your hips are very womanly and feminine."

"Womanly and feminine?"

"No doubt about it."

"The thighs?" she asked.

"In excellent taste," he assured her.

She sighed.

"Big ass though," she said. "I sat on your glasses."

"Yes," he said eagerly, "but you didn't *break* them. And your calves and ankles are fantastic. I even like your feet."

She brightened.

"I admit my feet are good. Everyone likes my feet." Then she collapsed, fell to brooding. "But that's all I've got—feet. Everything else is—well, nothing. You're just trying to make me feel better about myself."

"I'm not," he said. "I swear I'm not."

Then, his actor's instinct telling him the moment called for it, he struggled to his feet. He stood apart from her, legs planted solidly, hands thrust into his wet pockets. He lifted his chin, stared sternly out to sea.

"No, that's not true," he said. "I *was* trying to make you feel better. By telling you the truth. By telling you what you don't realize. That you're a very beautiful woman. Haven't other men told you that?"

"Yes," she said in a faint voice. "But only so they could fuck me."

"Oh."

"Do *you* want to fuck me?"

"I wish you wouldn't use that word," he said.

"Why not?"

"The night's too lovely."

"Oh yes," she breathed. "Yes. I understand exactly what you mean. I'm sorry."

"Oh, that's all right," he said cheerfully. He sat down again at her side. "The night's so incredible—that's all."

"I understand." She nodded.

"So incredible—that I want to fuck you."

"I want to fuck you, too. I belong to you; you saved my life."

"Oh no . . ."

"You did, you did!"

"Oh, just because I know a little French . . ." He shrugged modestly. "Don't feel you owe me anything. You don't."

"My life belongs to you," she said solemnly.

"You told me that was worthless."

"That was before you told me how beautiful I am. My nose. You didn't mention my nose."

"Your nose is divine," he said.

She sniffed, wiped her nose with the sleeve of his jacket.

"Right now it's running," she said.

"Running divinely," he said.

He slid an arm across her shoulders. He pulled her close, experimentally. She did not object.

"Do you really want to?" he asked. "Make love, I mean?"

She hestitated a moment, considering.

"Yes, I believe I do," she said finally. "I'm not certain, you understand, but I think I do."

"You don't have to, you know. I'm not a mad rapist."

"I know that, silly. I could run back into the ocean."

"Oh God, not again. But *why*? Do you want to make love, I mean? Or think perhaps you want to make love even if you're not absolutely certain?"

"Because you have ambition," she said.

"I do."

"And dreams."

"Plenty of those."

"I don't, you see," she said sorrowfully. But then she

brightened. "But maybe, just maybe, if we make love, I'll catch it from you."

"Catch what?"

"Well...you know who you are, what you want. Maybe I'll catch that if we make love. Through osmosis or something. Then I'll know who I am and what I want."

"Well..." he said doubtfully. "There's no guarantee, you know."

"I'm willing to take the chance. I *must* take the chance. Please?"

He was horrified, and looked at her sternly.

"Don't *ever* say 'Please' to me or any other man. You're too much of a woman to say 'Please.'"

"It's working!" she cried. "It's working!"

She wrestled out of David's jacket, tossed it aside. She rolled over atop him, pressing him back onto the sand. Crazed with lust, she began fumbling at his trousers.

"My glasses are steaming up," he told her.

"Damn, damn, damn!" she said furiously.

"What's wrong?"

"Your zipper is stuck. I think there's a piece of seaweed caught in it."

They both bent their heads over his stubborn fly, and eventually got it open. Then, with much awkwardness and flopping about, he grew naked also. In white moonlight and black shadow, they became part of the etched beach. They embraced, shivering, and kissed, kissed, kissed.

"The sand may hurt," he warned her. "It irritates, you know."

"I don't care."

"Let me spread out my jacket. We'll lie on that."

"It'll get all wrinkled."

"Who cares? I love you."

"It's a very nice tweed. I love you, too."

"Actually, the sleeves are a quarter-inch too long. You're so beautiful."

"I love tweed," she said. "It's so—so tweedy. Isn't that a funny word—tweedy? Say it three times."

"Tweedy, tweedy, tweedy," he said. "Yes, it is strange."

"Darling, are you cold?"

"Cold?" he said. "Me? Oh no. No."

"I thought you shivered."

"With delight. When you ran your fingernails down my back. The books say it takes time for a man and a woman to become sexually accustomed to each other."

"The books," she scoffed. "What do they know about it? I mean, if the *knew* about it, the writers, they'd be doing it instead of writing about it, wouldn't they? May I touch you?"

"If you wish."

"It's so strange," she said wonderingly.

He propped himself on his elbows, and they both stared down at him. In truth, it looked a bit odd, throbbing in the moonlight.

"How can men go through life with this hanging from them?" she asked. "It's really incredible."

"No more incredible than a woman's breasts. They hang too. Sometimes."

"Well, doesn't it get in the way? Doesn't it annoy you?"

"Not really. You get used to it."

"I suppose so," she said doubtfully. "What do you do with it when you sleep?"

"I mail it to Boston."

"Seriously," she insisted.

"Seriously, it's not a problem," he assured her. "What do women do with their breasts when they sleep?"

"Still...Look at it, David. It *is* strange."

"Like a turkey's neck?"

"Oh no. More like a sausage."

"A Vienna sausage?"

"Heavens, no!"

"Thank you," he said. "But not a salami, either."

"Look, David!" she cried. "It's growing!"

"I know," he said happily. "Perhaps it will become a kielbasy."

"What's that?"

"A hot Polish sausage."

"Yummy!" she said. "Still, when you think of it, David, if you were God and creating men and women, it would be very difficult to think of a better design."

"I can't think of one," he acknowledged.

"It's getting bigger, David!"

"Perhaps it's trying for a bologna. Does it frighten you?"

"No, not frighten...but it awes me. I'm very impressed."

"Thank you."

"Can you walk when it's like that?" she asked.

"Must I?"

"Of course not. I was just asking a question."

"Yes, I can walk. But I'd prefer not to. It looks silly."

"It doesn't look silly at all. It's sweet. Besides, it's for me, isn't it?"

"Oh yes," he vowed, "yes. It is yours. I hope you like it."

"I'm sure I shall," she said. "You know what I think we should do now?"

"I hope I guess right," he said.

"I think I should lie on my back," she said thoughtfully. "With my knees spread and lifted. And you must lie on top of me between my legs."

"I think that's a splendid idea," he said. "As soon as possible."

Not without difficulty, they rolled, lifted, and

plunged into the position she had prescribed. She stared at the moon over his left shoulder and winked at the man.

"Yes, David," she murmured. "That's just right... just right..."

"Am I too heavy on you?" he inquired solicitously.

"Gloriously heavy."

"You must never do that again," he said severely.

"I thought you liked it?"

"Suicide, I mean."

"Oh," she said. "Well... it brought us together."

"Enchanting suicide!" he said.

"Marvelous suicide!" she said. "David... my ears. You didn't mention my ears."

"I worship your ears," he gasped. "Fabulous, sexy ears," he grunted "I think I'm ready," he groaned.

"I know you're ready."

"Are you ready?"

"Oh so ready," she breathed.

"Well then... 'soft stillness and the night become the touches of sweet harmony.'"

"What is that?"

"*Merchant of Venice.* I was reciting it when I heard you cry out."

"David..."

"What?"

"Au secours!" she cried out. "Au secours! Aidez-moi! Aidez-moi!"

"I'll save you," he said, proving it.

"Oh yes!" She wept with bliss. "Oh yes! Save me, dear David, save me, save me...."

The bloated moon dwindled, dwindled, and lowered in the sky. It became no larger than an electric bulb illuminating the bare stage of the university theatre. Barbara Evings and David Marlow sat across the table from each other. His arm was extended, his hand covered one of hers.

"I remember, I remember." He smiled. "It was a wonderful night—a night full of wonders."

"We never had a night like that again," she said sadly.

"We had others just as good."

"Just as good," she said. "But—different."

He looked at her, the smile going from his eyes.

"Did it work, Barbara? Did you find out who you were that night?"

"Oh yes," She nodded. "I found out. That I loved you. I thought that would be enough for me."

He drew his hands away, sat back in his chair. He began to fiddle with the capped flask, spinning it on the tabletop. He stared down at the flashing silver.

"But it wasn't?" he asked. "Isn't?"

"Wasn't," she agreed gravely. "Isn't. Loving you isn't enough. I want more."

"You have all I have to give," he told her.

"I don't believe that."

"It's the truth."

"David, if I believed that, I'd walk back into the ocean, baby and all."

"Don't say that!" he cried.

"That *is* the truth. But don't worry. I won't do it. I have faith in you."

He glanced at her swiftly, then looked down again. He tried a short laugh, but it came out as a snort.

"I'm glad one of us does," he said.

"I do."

"You pretend you do," he told her.

"Can't you pretend?"

Now it was so complicated, they were both lost.

What did she want him to pretend—faith in himself? Or . . . ? He guessed correctly.

"Play at love?" he asked.

"Yes," she said promptly. "All right. Play the lover. Tell me I mean more to you than you do to yourself. Open up. Give yourself to me. Can't you do that?"

"Jesus Christ!" he said angrily. "You're as bad as Toby."

"Is it really so awful, David? To pretend, I mean? To play at loving me?"

"What would that accomplish—if we both knew I was playing a part?"

"It might become second nature to you," she said. "And then first nature."

"I don't believe that," he said, his voice echoing around the empty theatre. "Essence is created from within, not by outside influence. I cannot act what I cannot feel. That would be faking. And if I play a role with you, why not with everyone? Then Toby would be right, and Toby is not right. I proved that to him an hour ago. The essence of a man exists beyond playing parts. The ego is what makes a great creative actor."

"Toby says—" she started.

But she stopped when he slammed his fist down on the table. Then he grabbed up the flask, opened it, tilted his head backward. He drained it, then threw it skittering across the table to fall to the stage. Barbara bent slowly to pick it up.

"Toby, Toby, Toby!" he shouted furiously. "That's all I hear. The man is all old stories, dirty jokes, misquoted lines, fake angers, simulated loves, fictitious passions, and imagined memories. Everyone listens to Toby Marlow. Everyone believes Toby Marlow. But *he* is nothing. He doesn't exist."

Barbara continued calmly...

"Toby says players who feel as you do ignore communication just to massage their own egos. That you give pleasure to no one but yourself."

"I know what Toby thinks. I don't want to hear any more about it. I know what is true."

"Do you? Is that why you're frightened? David, I know now who I am. Do you know who you are?"

He folded his arms on the tabletop, leaned forward to hide his face. He and Barbara sat long moments in silence. Finally . . .

"What did you say?" she asked.

"Nothing," he said, his voice muffled. "I said nothing."

"Strange," she said. "I could have sworn I heard someone cry ever so faintly. 'Au secours! Au secours!'"

SCENE FOUR

THE MARLOW LIVING ROOM, almost dusted, was decorated for the wedding of Cynthia and Toby. A small, square pavilion had been erected in front of the fireplace. The fluttering walls were white nylon curtains; overhead was suspended an enormous white paper bell.

The remainder of the room was adorned with Japanese paper doves, paper fish, paper animals, and streamers hanging from beams, the ceiling electric fan, and lighting fixtures. Behind the couch, a rough table had been fashioned of planks laid across sawhorses.

The surface had been covered with sheets, and on display were bottles of beer, wine, and whiskey, buckets of ice, trays of food, baskets of fruit, a whole sliced ham, turkey, smoked trout, glasses, plates, cutlery, platters of bread, side dishes, desserts, pastries, etc. While not exactly groaning, this board was certainly whimpering softly.

Also prominent in this festive room were twenty (20! Count them! 20!) cardboard cutouts, five to six feet tall, standing upright on splayed wooden bases. They were the type of photographic cutouts (nauseously tinted) exhibited outside theatres, nightclubs, and burlesque houses. These two-dimensional statues were of actors and dancers, clowns and kings, whores, villains, saints, and comics. Showing more teeth than seemed humanly possible, standing immobile in exaggerated postures—but bobbing slightly in the wind of a live celebrant passing by—the cutouts gave the impression of a crowded room, a "cast of thousands," the hurly-burly of a jammed, excited scene.

Actually, as a keen-eye spectator would soon discern, the wedding congregation was a very small multitude. Present in the flesh were the bride and groom, Cynthia and Toby, standing in the pavilion hand in hand before the minister, who was nondenominational and nondescript. Also present were Jacob and Julius Ostretter, keeping as far apart as possible, and their practically identical wives—plump, jolly women with granite corsets, behived hairdos, and plenty of sequins. David Marlow and Barbara Evings stood close to the pavilion, dressed to the nines and solemn. In the background, a beaming Blanche, dressed to the tens, wept genially from much happiness and one small whiskey.

If the evening had been scored, it would have been marked con brio.

"And now," the minister intoned. "I pronounce you husband and wife. You may kiss the bride."

"Goddamn right!" Toby Marlow shouted.

He immediately embraced Cynthia passionately, bent her backward in a theatrical hug, and pressed his lips to hers like Rudolph Valentino giving the business to Nita Naldi. When he let her up for air, the eager minister rushed forward to kiss a surprised Cynthia on the lips. The others clustered about—David and Barbara, the Ostretters, and Blanche—to salute bride and groom with handshakes, hugs, kisses. And shouts and laughter . . .

"Bravo!"

"Congratulations!"

"Mazeltov!"

"May all your trouble be little ones!"

"Happiness forever!"

"Well done, well done!"

In the confusion, the minister sneaked to the end of the kissing line and was about to claim seconds. Toby pushed him away.

"Enough of sex!" he cried. "Now all I want to hear is the popping of corks! David, thou legal son, wilt thou do the honors?"

David and Blanche moved to the table behind the couch. Champagne bottles were taken from ice buckets, corks were extracted, goblets were filled and passed around in a buzz of excited chatter.

"Silence!" David shouted. "Silencio!"

When he had their attention, he raised his glass high.

"A toast!" Toby crowed. "A royal toast!"

"How *nice*!" Cynthia said.

"Ladies and gentlemen," David said, "I give you Mr. and Mrs. Toby Marlow, of whom I have the honor of being the fruit."

"Hear, hear!" Toby shouted.

"To my mother and father," said David. "Long may they wave!"

"Long may they wave!" came the answering roar, and glasses were drained, including those of Cynthia and Toby's. The latter immediately whirled and smashed his glass into the fireplace.

"Oh Toby!" Cynthia said. "Our best Waterford crystal!"

"The hell it was!" he said. "Just a five-and-ten glass—something I keep handy for dramatic gestures."

David and Blanche refilled the empty goblets.

Suddenly Dr. Ostretter's wife rushed to the tinny upright piano, seated herself, and began to bang out the wedding march, the recessional from the altar. Toby, champagne glass in hand, took Cynthia's hand under his arm, and the two, raising wine to the assembled company, made a grand parade about the room.

"Dear friends, dear friends," Toby caroled, "drink deep the nuptial cup and give us your blessings all! Let wassail proceed and joy be unrefined!"

Cynthia and Toby continued their tour, queen and king, bowing to the felicitations of their subjects and pausing to embrace and kiss, once more, David, Barbara, and Blanche.

"I beg you all," Toby shouted, "eat, drink, and make merry. For such a union as this was made in heaven, and tickets to witness the wild revelry of the marriage bed will go on sale shortly. It is, regrettably, a limited engagement."

Mrs. Ostretter, at the piano, launched into an enthusiastic but barely recognizable rendition of "Oh, how we danced on the night we were wed..." and Toby and Cynthia began waltzing about the room, soon to be joined by David and Barbara, Julius Ostretter and his wife, Dr. Jake and Blanche. The minister, smiling and nodding approvingly, made himself an enormous sandwich and filled a highball glass with champagne. He then moved over to the piano bench where his attentions to Mrs. Jacob Ostretter were something more (or less) than ecclesiastical.

Toby suddenly stopped dancing, withdrew from Cynthia's arms. He faced the carousing company, held up a hand for silence.

"Wait!" he yelled. "Wait! Stop the goddamned music! Listen to me!" Then, when they had quieted and looked at him expectantly, "Ladies and gentlemen—ruffians all!—in the excitement of this celebration and in my feverish hunger for what is to come, I almost forgot an important ceremony. Since I anticipate my wife's enthusiastic cooperation on our nuptial cot, I can safely term what I shall now display as this evening's piece de resistance. Ladies and gentlemen, my wedding gift to darling Cynthia!"

There was laughter, chatter, a spattering of applause as Toby darted from the room into the entrance hall. In the few moments he was gone, there were excited guesses as to what the gift would be.

Cynthia: "A black lace negligee!"

David: "An autographed photograph of himself!"

Barbara: "A collection of obscene limericks!"

Jacob: "A mink-covered pessary!"

Julius: "Last year's calendar!"

Blanche: "Six months' supply of horehound candy!"

But Toby ended their speculation by dashing back into the rowdy scene. He was carrying a gilded bird cage. Within was perched a rather scruffy mynah bird, squawking irritably at his treatment. Toby held up the cage before Cynthia.

"For you, darling," he said. "With everlasting devotion."

"Oh," she said, somewhat startled, "oh Toby, how nice. He—she—it's lovely. Thank you so much, dear."

"Now talk," Toby said.

"What shall I say?" Cynthia asked.

"No, no, not you," Toby said. "The bird. All right, now talk."

The bird squawked indignantly.

"'Speak the speech, I pray you,'" Toby entreated, "'as I pronounced it to you, trippingly on the tongue.'"

"Squawk!"

"Goddamn it," Toby said, "we rehearsed for hours! Will you, for Chrissake, say *something*? Anything!"

"Squawk!"

"Ahh, go fuck yourself," Toby said disgustedly.

"I love you, Cyn," the bird said clearly.

The company broke into cheers and loud applause, although David Marlow could be heard to mutter, "No motivation."

"Oh Toby," Cynthia said, "how truly *nice*!"

"I love you, Cyn," the bird said.

"What power!" Toby said proudly. "What feeling! What presence! What deep, heartfelt passion!"

"I love you, Cyn," the bird said. "I love you, Cyn. I love you, Cyn. I love—"

"All right already!" Toby yelled. "Shut up and eat a seed. It's my wedding gift to you, darling. The birds of the sky—and even of the cage—know and respect and echo my emotions. I love you, Cyn."

There were more laughs, cheers, and applause from the miniature mob. The cardboard cutouts bobbed approvingly.

"And I love you, Toby," Cynthia said. "And here is my wedding gift to you."

She lifted the lid of the upright piano, extracted a small package wrapped in white tissue paper and tied with a blue ribbon. She presented it to Toby and kissed his bald head. The guests watched expectantly as he tore the paper away frantically.

"What is it, what is it?" he said. "It's heavy! Maybe it's a five-pound box of money!"

He discarded the wrappings on the floor. In his hands, revealed, was an ornately carved wooden box, a music box. Toby looked up at Cyn a moment, looked down again, and slowly raised the lid. The silent, entranced audience heard a low whir of machinery, and then the plinked melody of what sounded like a hopelessly old-fashioned, sentimental, rinky-tink vaudeville tune. Toby roared with laughter, and shouting, "You remembered, you remembered!," clasped Cynthia to him and kissed lips, cheeks, eyes, hair, and whatever additional morsels came within reach.

Finally, gasping from his efforts, he held her away and gazed fondly into her eyes.

"How wonderful! Cyn, it must have cost a fortune!"

"What is it?"

"What is it?"

"What's playing?"

"What the hell is that?"

"I don't recognize it."

"What's the song?"

Toby held up both palms and patted them toward his audience, shushing them.

"Lydies and gents, you are hearing a tender work of musical art I had the honor of singing before the crowned heads of Europe and the bald heads of America on the vaudeville stage more years ago than I care to remember. It's called 'Go Into the Roundhouse, Nellie; He'll Never Corner You There,' and as soon as the melody comes around again, I will be pleased to favor you with one stanza and one refrain."

The company waited happily; Toby set the opened music box on the table. He then assumed an exaggerated posture of fear and despair, the back of one hand pressed to his brow, the other arm extended, palm held up beseechingly. He awaited his musical cue; the others were silent and attentive. Then he began singing:

"At last the mother saw her child
"Flee thru the stormy night;
"And close behind her ran the fiend
"Who gave her such a fright.
"The mother cried aloud in pain,
"And prayed with all her might:"
(Refrain)
"Go into the roundhouse, Nellie;
"He'll never corner you there.
"Go into the roundhouse, Nellie,
"And put your faith in prayer.
"The world is cruel and heartless,
"But keep your virtue fair-r-r.
"Go into the roundhouse, Nellie;
"He'll nev-v-ver co-o-o-or-r-rner you there!"

Toby bowed low after this touching rendition, which had been complete with broad expressions and elocutionary gestures. His audience broke into wild applause.

"Bravo!"

"Encore!"

"More! More!"

"Marvelous!"

"What a performance!"

"Bravissimo!"

Toby held up a hand modestly.

"Enough, dear friends. Always leave them laughing when you say good-by."

"Oh, I want to get married again and again and again!" Cynthia exclaimed. "It's so much *fun*!"

"And so we shall, luv!" Toby shouted, to be heard above the hubbub. "A Jewish wedding, and a Catholic wedding, and a Buddhist wedding, and a Cherokee wedding. As long as weddings and our days shall last. Every day a new marriage, a new ceremony, and one more orgy until the wine runs dry!"

The jollity resumed. People ate, people drank; there was purposeless movement; groups formed and disbanded, conversations ended as quickly as they began; laughter, shouting, kisses, spilled drinks, and broken glasses.

The minister wandered over to the mynah's cage. Looking about slyly to make certain he was unobserved, he poured whiskey into the bird's drinking cup. Then he watched, nodding approvingly as the bird poked its beak experimentally into the liquid.

The rhinestoned lady at the piano launched into a Greek-inspired tune ("Never on a Sunday..."). Toby immediately shook out a handkerchief, held one corner, handed the other to David. Father and son did a slow, graceful Greek dance, bobbing and dipping. Occasionally they slapped their thighs and shouted, "Yah!"

"What a pleasure to watch!" Dr. Jacob Ostretter said.

"Two grown men dancing together?" Lawyer Julius Ostretter demanded. "That's a pleasure to you?"

"Who asked you, moron?" Jacob said.

"Who are you calling moron?" Julius said. "You idiot—which happens to be worse than a moron."

"I don't like your tone," Jacob said.

"I don't like your manner," Julius said.

"With your taste," Jacob said, "that's a compliment."

"Quack!" Julius said.

"Shyster!" Jacob said.

"I warn you," Julius said, "you go too far!"

"You can't go far enough!" Jacob said.

"I dare you to strike me!" said Julius.

"I double-dare *you*!" said Jacob.

The Greek dance of Toby and David had stopped. The music had stopped. The guests had quieted and were now watching this confrontation with fascination. As Jacob and Julius bristled, moved closer to each other, butted their paunches, the others, including their delighted wives, formed a circle about the increasingly red-faced combatants.

"I slap your face!" Julius shouted.

He did so.

"I slap yours!" Jacob shouted.

He did so.

"I twist your nose!" Julius screamed.

He did so.

"I twist yours!" Jacob screamed.

He did so.

Puffing furiously, tears in their eyes from their wrenched proboscises, the brothers jammed closer to each other, their arms cocked, hands clenched and held up awkwardly.

"I'll demolish you!" Julius shrieked.

"I'll destroy you!" Jacob shrieked.

They swung simultaneously, thumping each other ineffectually on the upper arms. Then suddenly they were grappling, roaring with anger, huffing, groaning. They came down with a heavy thud, clasped in each other's arms, trying to strike blows. They rolled about, dust rising, and a chair, end table, and several cardboard cutouts went over with a crash.

Suddenly galvanized, but almost helpless with laughter, the remainder of the company pounced on the panting pugilists and pried them apart. Jacob and Julius were hauled protesting to their feet, soothed, patted, hair and clothing straightened. Then they were led away to opposite corners of the room, still glaring at each other, shaking fists, yelling blood-curdling Yiddish curses.

"Wonderful!" Toby cried, wiping his eyes. "How wonderful! Darling, our wedding bash is a success. A fight!"

"Oh Toby!" Cynthia said. "Please, please, all of you! No fights and no arguments on this of all nights."

Toby embraced her.

"You're right, Cyn—as usual. No fights, no disagreements, no deep, deep thoughts on this, the happiest of all occasions, thou fairest of the fair!"

The party regained its festive spirit. The minister interrupted his gorging long enough to replenish the whiskey in the bird's emptied water cup (thereby contributing to the delinquency of a mynah). David and Barbara fed each other tidbits from the wedding feast. Blanche and Mrs. Julius Ostretter arm-wrestled on the cocktail table. The Ostretter brothers, keeping carefully apart, wandered about, morosely munching on sandwiches.

Mrs. Jacob Ostretter, back at the piano, began playing a lively Irish jig. Blanche left off arm-wrestling, leapt to her feet and, champagne goblet in hand, began to dance, capering, skirt held high. The others circled around her, laughing, drinking, eating, a few clapping in time to the music.

"Higher!" Cynthia called. "Higher!"

"Take it off!" the minister yelled. "Take it off!"

"Put it on!" David yelled. "Put it on!"

"Pink drawers!" Toby marveled, watching Blanche cavort. "I swear to God, pink drawers! Oh Cyn, dear Cyn, let me marry this marvelous woman too. Canst thou not share me?"

"Of course, sweet Toby," she said. "Whomever your loving heart desires."

"Barbara, too," Toby said. "And every woman and

man in this room and in the whole wide world. I wish to
wed you all and bed you all and enter into all of you,
and you shall enter into me!"

"I love sin!" the mynah squawked, obviously
inebriated. "I love sin!"

Silenced for a moment by this shocking outburst,
the guests soon responded with laughter and applause.
The bird was fed crumbs from the table, his drinking
cup replenished with champagne, his cage decorated
with paper streamers.

The lady at the piano began something slow and
sentimental.

David put his arms about Barbara's swollen waist,
his fingers dangling on her ass. She clasped her hands
behind his neck. They shuffled their feet in time to the
music, moving in a very small circle.

"Love me?" he asked.

"Hate you," she said.

"I hate you, too. For the last time, will you marry
me?"

"For the last time, no."

"Because I'm me?"

"Because you're not you," she said.

"I'm all there is," he said. "There isn't any more."

"There is!" she insisted. "There is!"

"Dreamer!" he scoffed.

"You taught me that," she told him.

They stopped dancing and drew apart a little,
staring bravely into each other's eyes. Slowly their
hands unclasped, fell to their sides. They moved farther
apart, still staring. Toby, rushing by with a slice of
naked ham in one hand, an opened bottle of beer in the
other, saw their solemn estrangement. He skidded to a
halt, looked from one to the other.

"What's this, kids?" he demanded. "What's this?
Where is the bloom of roses in those happy cheeks?
Where is the gleam of California whites in those

delighted smiles? What the fuck is going on?"

David said, "The lady said no—again."

"I told you you were a lousy player," Toby said. "How did you ask her?"

"I said, 'Barbara, will you marry me?'"

"Barbara, is that what he said?" Toby asked her in disbelief.

"Yes."

"Nothing more?" he persisted.

"Nothing more."

"Dolt!" Toby said to David. "Must I play Cyrano to your Christian? Tell Barbara you love her. Go ahead—tell her!"

"Barbara, I love you."

"'Barbara, I love you,'" Toby mimicked. "Ye gods and little fishes! Have you learned nothing from me? Nothing at all? Now listen to this.... Barbara, darling... I know better than you what I am, and how far short I fall from the man you dreamed you might love and hoped you might marry. I know only too well that I am dull and withdrawn and locked up in my own ego. I know I have little capacity for joy. I don't have any small talk, and I have moods of gloom when there is no living with me. I know that I am opinionated and frequently pompous. But I—"

"Hey, wait a minute!" David said. "You can't—"

"But Barbara," Toby continued without a pause, "there is one thing I do have, overflowing and without end. And that is my love for you. That love makes up for all my faults, those I know and those I don't. It is a love so enormous, so overwhelming, that it carries the power to correct my faults, to teach me passion, to make me a new man and make you a new life. I beg you to be blinded by the love I have for you. As a brilliant sun casts everything in a golden radiance, so my love for you will make our life together warm and glowing. Barbara, wilt thou marry me?"

"Yes," she said promptly, "I will."

"And that, my imbecile son," Toby said to David, "is how it's done. Now get on the goddamn ball, prune-wit!"

Toby trotted away to join the gaiety. Barbara and David were left alone, still staring at each other sadly. They turned, busied themselves at the table, selecting food, mixing drinks.

"You can't say that, can you?" she asked. "What Toby said?"

"No, I can't," he said coldly. "I told you; I won't pretend. I won't be a player."

"Have you tried the smoked trout?" she asked.

The music increased, in tempo and volume; the party whirled on with laughter, bursts of song, solo dances, increasingly amorous embraces. Then Toby mounted a chair, held up a commanding hand. When the piano and company fell silent, he declaimed:

"'If music be the food of love, play on! Give me excess of it, that, surfeiting, the appetite may sicken, and so die. That strain again! It had a dying fall; O! it came o'er my ear like the sweet sound that breathes upon a bank of violets, stealing and giving odour!'"

All entranced and then applauding:

"Bravo! Bravo!"

"Well done!"

"Beautiful, just beautiful!"

"There's no one like Toby Marlow!"

"More! More!"

"Encore!"

The mad music, the dancing, the eating, the drinking—all took up again. It was Breughel's "The Wedding Feast"—without codpieces. Toby was dancing by himself now, caught up in some secret dream that only he could recognize. Cynthia and Blanche danced together in a formal, faintly smiling and faintly drunken delight. The minister sat alongside Mrs.

Jacob Ostretter on the piano bench, rubbing his wine-stained lips along her bare shoulder. More glasses had been spilled, more food dropped. Barbara and David circled each other aimlessly, waiting. . . . Jacob and Julius advanced and retreated, wary cocks looking for an opening to strike.

"A reel!" Toby shouted suddenly. "A reel! Musician, I will have a reel! King Toby commands a reel!"

Obediently the pianist launched into a spirited, if off-key version of "Turkey in the Straw." The entire company, with fumblings and stumblings and lurchings, joined hands and began gamboling in a rough circle about the couch and dining table. They shouted. "Da-da-diddle-diddle-da;   da-da-diddle-diddle-da," and similar nonsense just to keep time to the raw music. It grew faster and louder, all caught up in a joy too frantic to contain, until...

. . . until Toby Marlow stopped dancing, dropped hands, uttered a scream of such pain and anguish that the others shivered and were brought to a halt. The music ended on a crushing chord. They all turned to stare at Toby as, clutching a chair arm, he slid slowly, tragically to the floor. They were too shocked, too stunned to come to his aid. He was obviously in pain he could hardly endure, but he could not—*could not*—pass up the opportunity for a theatrical gesture. His arm rose slowly from his side; a trembling finger pointed at a startled Dr. Jacob Ostretter.

"Goddamn you, Jake!" Toby gasped. "You promised me a run of six months, and now you're sending me out on the road, and I don't want to go. Wait till Equity hears about this!"

ACT THREE

SCENE ONE

THE MARLOWS' BEDROOM had undergone changes and
taken on the appearance of a sickroom. Extra bolsters
had been added to the unmade bed, and the churned
blankets and rumpled sheets were littered with books,
magazines, an opened box of candy, a torn bag of
popcorn, etc. Next to the bed was a tall tank of oxygen,
with attached tube and mask. Alongside the oxygen
tank, on the floor, was a half-empty bottle of whiskey.

The shades were drawn; the chandelier and lamp
were lighted. There were several bouquets in the room,
in vases, in various stages of decay. On a small table
was a collection of medical supplies: bottles of pills,

towels, basins, a plastic container of ice, a hot-water bottle, etc. Also a decanter of wine and a box of cigars.

Toby Marlow was seated in a wheelchair near the drum table. He was covered to the waist with a plaid comforter. He was paler, drawn, and his speech had become somewhat slurred. But he hadn't lost any of his defiance, and talked as rapidly and loudly as ever. But now he had a tendency to splutter, and wiped his lips frequently with tissues plucked from a box he held on his lap. He dropped the used tissues onto the floor; they surrounded him like a snowfall. A heavy cane was hooked over the arm of his wheelchair.

David Marlow was seated in the leather club chair on the other side of the drum table. He wore his usual conservative business suit, with vest, and the horn-rimmed spectacles. He was consulting his playscript, leafing through it to find the speech he wanted. He too seemed thinner, tense, paler.

"Toby, are you sure you're up to this?" he asked.

"Yes, I'm up to this, sonny boy," Toby snarled. "There's nothing wrong with me a little death won't cure. So what's eating your director?"

"I don't know," David said. "I honestly don't know. He keeps saying, 'You're fine, David; you're doing fine.' But I get a take on him, and I don't think he thinks I'm doing fine. I think he thinks I'm a one-man catastrophe. But he can't verbalize it. He can't tell me what I'm doing wrong."

"Goddamn it," Toby said disgustedly. "I know I suffer from verbal diarrhea, but do you think still water runs deep? The hell it does! Still water runs stupid. Your director can't say what he wants because he doesn't *know* what he wants. He may feel it, but he can't put it into words? So what good is it? Words are everything. They're beautiful. Sublime. Where the fuck would we be without lovely words? Unexpressed ideas and emotions last as long as a fart in a keg of nails.

What words have you been working on?"

"The big soliloquy," David told him. "'To be or not to be.' Toby, that's a bitch."

"I know, I know." His father nodded. "In a speech as long as that, the first thing you've got to do is get your breathing right. Unless you've got the breathing and timing and pauses, you've got nothing. After you learn to get through it without panting like you've been running a four-minute mile, then you can start thinking about what the hell you're talking about. Have you got the breathing?"

"Yes, I've got the breathing and the timing and the beats. But I can't get a hook on it. I don't know what's going on. There's no logic to that speech."

"No logic?" Toby shouted. "Thou devil's spawn! Listen, Will was a poet before he was a playwright. Since when do you expect logic from a poet? You're lucky if you get decent table manners. I know about these things. I'm something of a poet myself."

"I know," David said resignedly. "I've heard your limericks."

"I'd call you a son of a bitch if I didn't respect your mother so much. Get me a big Scotch on ice."

"Toby, you're drinking too much."

"Balls."

"How many drinks do you have a day?"

"Who the hell counts?"

"Come on, Toby—how many?"

"Ten. Twelve. Something like that."

"Can't you cut that in half?" David asked earnestly.

"All right," Toby said. "I will."

"You will?" David said, astonished. "Five or six drinks a day?"

"Sure," Toby cackled. "All doubles."

"Doctor Jake said—"

"Fuck Doctor Jake!" Toby said furiously. "It's my goddamn pancreas! 'Pancreas.' Jesus Christ, what a

.word to do in a king. It's as humiliating as choking to death on a toothpick. Now get me that drink or I'll crawl across the floor on my belly and die at your feet like Leslie Howard in *The Petrified Forest*."

Sighing, David put his playscript aside and retrieved the bottle of Scotch next to the oxygen tank. He poured a dollop into a medicine glass, added ice and a little water. He stirred the drink with a thermometer, wondering which type it was and not really caring. He brought the whiskey to Toby.

"Go ahead, kill yourself," he said. "I don't care if you live or not."

Toby took a deep swallow. Then, trembling, with clawed hands, he began to play an old codger.

"Oh God bless you, boy, God bless you! You warm the heartles of my cock. Oh, you're so kind to your feeble old father."

"You're not the easiest father in the world to live with."

"So?" Toby said, straightening up. "Who gave you guarantees? The Declaration of Independence says you can *pursue* happiness; it doesn't say anything about catching it."

"I think I'll have a little drink," David said.

"Smartest thing you've done all day."

David went back to the medicine table and began busying himself with Scotch and water.

"I owe you an apology," he mumbled.

"What?" Toby said. "Speak up, for Chrissake."

"I owe you an apology!" David roared.

"So does God," Toby said. "What's yours for?"

"When I said I don't care if you live or not. I do care."

Toby didn't say anything. He watched David move across the room back to the club chair. David sat on the edge of the chair, hunched over, his glass held between his knees. The playscript was on the floor. David nudged it with his toe.

"I just don't feel it," he said miserably. "The soliloquy, I mean."

"I know that. And your director knows it."

"Well... what's my motivation?"

Toby sighed wearily, took a mouthful of his drink, put his head back, gargled a moment, then swallowed it.

"I don't know what your motivation is, mutton-head. For that speech or for wanting to be a player."

"An actor," David said mechanically. "I don't play at it."

"You sure as hell don't."

There were several moments of silence while they nibbled slowly at their drinks. They didn't look at each other. Occasionally Toby's eyes closed, but only for an instant. He seemed to force them open by conscious will.

"Listen, Toby," David said hesitantly. "I have a wonderful idea on how that 'To be or not to be' speech should be given."

"Oh? What's that?"

"I want to deliver it with my back to the audience."

"Your back to the audience?"

"Yes. It's obviously a very intellectual, introspective contemplative speech, and the actor should do nothing by expression or gesture to detract from the words."

"Uh-huh." Toby nodded. "And what does your director think of this wonderful idea?"

"Well, ah, I haven't told him yet."

"Before you do, I have an even better idea for you. Why appear onstage at all? Why not record the speech on tape, and all the stage manager has to do is turn it on. You could be out having a beer and a giant McDonald's hamburger."

"You don't have to get snotty about it."

"I knew you were an imbecile, but I didn't think you were a coward. Turn your back on the audience for that speech? Heavens to Betsy, you poor little bantling, that's a cop-out. You're scared shitless of this one, aren't you?"

"I don't know," David muttered. "That's the problem. I don't know what I'm supposed to do. What I'm supposed to feel."

"What *you* feel?" Toby hooted. "Triple-damned egotist!"

"You're the biggest egotist of all!" David yelled at him.

"The hell I am! I give myself as much as I can, and give and give and give, and screw my motivation and diddling my ego; it doesn't mean a thing to me." He stopped suddenly, took a deep swallow of his drink, chewed a few fragments of ice. Then he drew a deep breath. "All right. Let's calm down. Let me try once more—just once more. David, you've got to admit we're all sad shits. Ninety-nine percent of all the people in the world are sad, sad shits. We're all failures in one way or another. We lie and we cheat and we rob and we betray, and we act in a million other awful ways. God, we're such small, crawling things! We're not even animals! Animals don't do the things we do. What animals torture and kill for kicks? So fucking *awful*! But occasionally someone like Willie Shakespeare comes along and shows us what we might be. And not only poets and playwrights, but novelists and artists, and sculptors and musicians, and scholars and saints—and maybe a few raggedy-assed players in there. Not showing us what we *are*, but what we might be. What in God's name do you think art is all about? It shows us what we could be: princes and kings, princesses and queens, nobles and courtiers, beautiful people of dignity and resolve. Heroes! Jesus Christ, we can be heroes! Do you know what that means? Do you realize what hope that offers? That we can all, each of us, aspire to something we know we are not. That's why Will wrote that long soliloquy, why he opened up Hamlet's mind and showed us his deepest thoughts— to link Hamlet with humanity, to make everyone who reads or hears those words feel an affinity for the Prince of Denmark, and so feel larger and better and grander, and forget, for a few minutes, that he's a sad, sad shit who cheats on his wife and betrays his best friend, or sells out his dreams, and he's going to die no smarter than he was born, never knowing what it was all about. So when you deliver that speech, you've got to open up. You've got to rip yourself open, split yourself wide. You're not only the Prince of Denmark; you're Everyman. And you've got to give everyone in the audience a sense of the possibility of dignity and meaning in life."

"Does it exist?" David asked wonderingly.

"Does what exist?"

"Does life have dignity and meaning?"

"You infant!" Toby said pityingly. "Did you have your pap this morning? Of course life doesn't have dignity and meaning, you witless wonder. But you've got to pretend that it does. How else can you endure?"

"I want to be an actor. But I don't want to pretend."

"I've been pretending all my life," Toby said, "but I've just come to realize it. Nothing like a death sentence to make a man a philosopher. And while I'm giving your so-called brain the massage it needs, there's something else I want to straighten you out on. But first build me a drink. And take it easy on the ice: I'm not a corpse—yet."

Obediently, David took Toby's glass back to the medicine table. There was a moment of panic when both realized the whiskey bottle was empty. But terror was averted when a new bottle was discovered in the cellaret of the drum table. David poured their drinks with a heavy hand.

"Water?" he asked.

"Not too much. Peeing isn't one of my favorite pastimes these days."

They sat back, relaxed and smiling, holding their glasses up to each other a brief moment before taking the first swallow.

"I've decided what I want on my tombstone," Toby announced.

"What's that?"

"'Here lies Toby Marlow, stiff at last.'"

"Not bad." David laughed. "But how about: 'I'm only pretending'?"

"Bravo!" Toby said. "Every now and then I think there may be some hope for you."

"What did you want to tell me?" David said.

"About what?"

"I don't know. But you said there was something you wanted to straighten me out on."

"I did? Now what the hell was it . . . ?"

"About Barbara?"

"Don't prompt me, goddamn it," Toby snarled. "No, Barbara wasn't involved. Now—oh, I've got it. See—the famous Marlow memory is still working; it's just slowing down, that's all. It's about what we talked about before. When—"

"We talked about a lot of things," David said.

"Will you stop flapping your flatulent mouth and let me finish? I said—that night we took a walk along the park—I said all of us—not only players but *everyone*— plays many, many roles in a lifetime, suiting the part to the other performer, whether it be onstage or off. And that good playing was a matter of style which, essentially, is having a good bag of tricks. Then, at the theatre, when we were rehearsing the 'O! that this too too solid flesh . . .' speech, you said I was wrong because the good players are—"

"The great actors," David interrupted.

"All right, the great actors. You said, in effect, that there was—there was . . . What the hell's wrong with me? I can't remember what I wanted to say."

"Probably the Scotch," David said casually.

"Never affected me like this before," Toby said, troubled. "I played a year of *Rain* dead drunk and never missed a cue. Where was I?"

David wanted to end this, seeing his father's tiredness, but could think of no graceful or easy way to withdraw. He took a gulp of his drink and plunged ahead. . . .

"I said, when we were rehearsing that speech, that you were wrong in believing that life is all pretending and great acting just a matter of tricks. I said you were wrong because great actors remain themselves no matter what part they're playing. With Olivier, Robards, Richardson, Scott, Gielgud, or any other star, we never forget who they are no matter what role they play. In other words, their ego and essence come across, come through the lines and action of the play. And the proof of that is that Olivier's Hamlet would be different from Richardson's, just as Garrick's Othello would be different from Irving's. So there's more to it than just tricks; it's the truth of the man that commands our respect. He knows who he is, and he projects that on the stage and by so doing, moves us and convinces us and reveals to us his truth. That's what I said."

"So you said, so you said." Toby nodded, obviously weary now. "And I've been thinking about it. I really have. And . . ."

"Toby, maybe we better cut this short. I've got to get to the theatre."

"No, no, don't go yet. I've got to tell you this while it's on my mind. No good on my mind. Words are

everything. The beautiful words. The sound of them!
The taste of them! Because you're wrong, you see. I've
been thinking about it, and I know now why you're
wrong. Because those great players are not revealing to
us what you call their ego and essence. Oh no. Now
each of us has an image of himself—who he is and what
he is. I, for instance, think I'm the greatest player who
ever lived. Another man might fancy himself as a great
lover, or a great statesman, or a great general, who is
only prevented by chance, bad luck, or circumstance
from revealing his genius to the world. We all have this
self-image, and we try to play the part as best we can.
You get it? We pretend we are the man we'd like to be.
All of us. Everyone. We've got this illusion of who we
are, and we act the part. Sometimes we even dress the
part. The closer reality comes to our dream, the
happier we are. But no one totally succeeds. It is still
pretend. It is all playing."

"I don't get it," David said. "What's that got to do
with great actors? With the stars?"

"Everything. It's got everything to do with them.
Because what you call their ego and essence, the truth
they reveal on the boards, is the part they are playing
for themselves! Now do you get it? What they project
on the stage is not their ego and essence; it's their vision
of themselves, a part they've been playing all their lives
and play so well that it convinces everyone. But it's still
all illusion. *Their* illusion."

"Wait a minute," David said slowly. "Are they
convinced that the part they're playing is actually
them?"

"No," Toby said. "Well . . . maybe. The stupid ones
might convince themselves that they're genuine and
not playing. But the smart ones, like me, lie awake at
three in the morning and know who they are. They
know then they're not the greatest players in the world,
and the face they present to the public is as false as if

they were wearing makeup and a nylon beard."

"Are you telling me that all great actors are playing a part *in addition* to the role they're playing onstage?"

"Right!" Toby shouted, nodding like a madman. "Now you've got it! They're so good at pretending, at *playing*, that they've created a part of their own, what you call their ego and essence. And not only great players. But everyone. Everyone does it. But it's all illusion, all dreaming. And the smart ones know it."

"Do you know it? About yourself?"

"Sure," Toby said genially. "I'm smart."

"All right," David said. "If you're not the greatest actor—or player—in the world, who are you?"

"Who am I? Who am I? I'll tell you who I am."

"That's what I want to hear," David said. "Tell me."

Toby began his next speech haltingly, almost diffidently. But his voice gained strength and resolution as he proceeded, the marvelous organ tones booming out. Finally he was speaking with fervor, as if shucking off a burden he had carried along too long and was now happy to be rid of, knowing how it freed him. His physical actions enforced his words. He began the speech seated in the wheelchair. He rose, let the plaid comforter fall to the floor. He used the cane to stalk about the room, keeping his face turned to David, never taking his eyes from him. When he reached his peroration, he threw the cane from him and ended with arms flung wide, standing triumphant, feet braced, chest outthrust, head up. It was a bravura.

"I," he began, "I am a—a charming buffoon. But there is a—a self-assurance about me that convinces. Yes. You may begin by laughing at me, but you end up impressed. I *convince*. Yes, I am a 'character' and glory in it. And if you don't like it, fuck you! Constantly drinking, constantly smoking, constantly flirting, I succeed at once in exemplifying and caricaturing a 'dirty old man.' As if there was any other kind!

"Every conversation, every gesture, every body movement, every expression, every action and reaction is not so much calculated as practiced. I am a natural player, my instincts sharpened by more than forty years of stage experience. Everything from Shakespeare to burlesque and back again. I have little knowledge of or interest in abstract ideas, except as they affect the theatre. But I have the gut aptitudes and the understanding of human frailties of the born survivor.

"I am shrewd rather than intelligent. But there is a streak of meanness in me. I come perilously close to being a grotesque. I am given to sudden furies, over as quickly as they begin. I am a poseur. I have played so many roles that I have never quite decided if I prefer playing hero or villain.

"I cheerfully insult family and friends. I fight with acquaintances and strangers, bullying, shouting, screaming, shouldering my way through life, striking before I can be struck. But if I must take blows, I give them back trebled. I enjoy being ribald. Maybe vulgar. Sometimes obscene.

"I am larger than life, but there is a little boy's swagger about me. Perhaps you have glimpsed something uncertain and fearful beneath my braggadocio. I know you have to work at liking me—I can be wearing, I suppose—but I can be so inimitable and charming, when I want to be, that all are my slaves. Do they recognize something in me, perhaps a heroic quality, they cannot find in themselves?

"Finally, I am a physical coward with a terror of death that no one knows except myself. And I will die nobly without revealing it, so fearful am I of being scorned or, worse yet, ignored. I know I am not a giant theatrical talent. But surely, after my passing, there is one person in the world, somewhere, who might one day say, 'He did very well with what he had.'"

As this speech progressed, David had been impressed, then shocked by Toby's apparent honesty. Toward the end, he rose to his feet in unconscious homage, surrendering completely to Toby's skill and intensity.

Toby concluded with a rather hokey shtick of letting his arms fall limply to his sides, bowing his head, allowing his entire frame to slump in resignation and defeat. Then, in the unendurable silence, David made a choked cry deep in his throat. He gathered up his playscript, rushed from the room. Toby remained in his "defeated" position until the door slammed behind his son.

Then Toby slowly raised his head, looked about cautiously. He stretched, smiled mysteriously. He moved to the medicine table, mixed a heavy drink. He shook two pills from a bottle onto his palm, popped them into his mouth, washed them down with a swallow of Scotch. He returned to the wheelchair, sat down, pulled up the comforter, tucked himself in. He was sitting serenely, sipping his drink, when Blanche entered without knocking.

"Ah, Ma Barker!" Toby said. "Just in time. Light me a cigar."

"You know what the doctor—" she started.

"I know what the goddamn doctor said, Madame LaFarge. Would you deny a dying man his last request?"

"Seems to me you have these 'last requests' every hour on the hour."

"Cut the shit and pour yourself a drink," he told her. "And light us a cigar."

Blanche mixed a highball for herself. Then she lighted a cigar, taking it from the box on the drum table. After she got it drawing smoothly, she handed it over to Toby, standing before him.

"Now what?" she asked. "Sure you don't want a

Welsh rarebit or pickled onions as a last request? Maybe you're as pregnant as Barbara."

"You go to hell," he said affably. "Babe, tell me something honestly, will you?"

"Have I ever faked you?" she asked.

"No, God bless you, you never have. Tell me—who am I?"

She looked at him, bewildered.

"You're Toby Marlow," she said.

"Toby Marlow?" he cried. "By God, I'll pretend I am! It's a marvelous part!"

She still looked at him, then shrugged, but finally smiled at his obvious good spirits. They raised their glasses in an unspoken toast. They handed the cigar back and forth.

SCENE TWO

THE MARLOWS' LIVING ROOM had also taken on the appearance of a sickroom. Medical supplies and pill bottles were set out on the cocktail table. A small tank of oxygen, with mask, stood near the couch. Toby's wheelchair, with cane hooked over one arm, was nearby. A battered guitar with a broken and coiled string leaned against the liquor cart.

Toby Marlow was, apparently, asleep on the couch. At least he was stretched out, covered with a throw quilt. And yet, during the following conversation, his eyes opened on occasion, he winced, grimaced, made certain small gestures with his hands atop the coverlet.

In other words, the old bastard was faking his sleep, eavesdropping on the talk of the two women in the room.

Cynthia was in her armchair, patiently doing needlework by the light of a gooseneck floor lamp. Barbara Evings, mostly in shadow, sat on the floor, knees drawn up and spread to accommodate her swollen belly. Occasionally she turned her head sideways to rest her cheek on a knee, looking more than ever like a dreamy Burne-Jones portrait.

It was early evening. The light from the windows was soft, violet, at once melancholy and restful. It was a time for quiet talk and sweet remembrances. Voices were low; the rhythm of conversation was slowed, almost contemplative....

"Oh..." Cynthia said regretfully, "I do believe I've dropped a stitch."

"Is it serious?" Barbara Evings asked.

"Oh no. Just a row. I'm so bad at counting. Did you see Doctor Jake today, dear?"

"Yes, I saw him."

"And what did he say?"

"I'm too skinny. I'm supposed to take vitamins and drink eggnog and eat regular meals."

"Very good." Cynthia nodded approvingly. "Toby has an excellent recipe for eggnog. It has rum and whiskey and brandy in it. It's delicious."

"I don't know," Barbara said doubtfully. "I think Doctor Jake meant just plain eggnog, without any alcohol in it."

"Really, dear? I'm not sure you can make it without whiskey. I must ask Blanche; she'll know. What else did he say?"

"Oh...nothing much. I'm a little run-down but generally in good shape. And I have an unexpectedly wide pelvis. I never knew that."

Cynthia looked up, concerned.

"It doesn't bother you, does it?"

"Of course not, Cynthia. Why should it?"

"Well, I once knew a woman who had three kidneys, and it bothered *her;* I don't know why. I thought it was rather a mark of distinction."

"Tomorrow I go to the obstetrician. Jake says he's very young and wealthy."

"That's nice, dear," Cynthia said, comforted. "I wouldn't want you going to a *poor* obstetrician. Did you see David today?"

"Cynthia, is Toby really asleep?"

"Of course he is, dear; can't you see? There are little bubbles on his lips. That means he's asleep."

"He's probably pretending."

"He may very well be. But it's not important, is it? Well, did you?"

"Did I what?"

"See David today."

"Oh. No. I've been sleeping so much lately, and he had gone to rehearsal when I got up. Then he came home for lunch while I was at the doctor's. And now I'm here, and he's gone again. But he left me a note."

Cynthia left off her sewing and looked up with interest, peering at Barbara over her spectacles.

"A note? Oh, I'm so glad, dear. What did it say?"

Barbara took a folded piece of paper from her bodice, opened it, craned to read it by the dim light from Cynthia's lamp.

"It says: 'Got to run. Rehearsal till late. Wait up if you can. Marry me. David.'"

"Isn't that *nice!* Such a *loving* note! Are you going to?"

"Wait up for him?" Barbara said. "I might."

"No, dear. Marry him."

"No," Barbara said determinedly. "I've made up my mind. I'm not going to."

"But you *love* him!"

"I don't, I *don't*!"

Cynthia's steadily moving hands came to rest. She disentangled her fingers. She leaned forward to stroke the girl's hair.

"Oh dear, dear, I may not be a very intelligent woman, but I do *feel* things, you know. And I feel you love David."

Suddenly Barbara began to weep audibly. She bent forward, buried her face in her hands, and sobbed, sobbed, sobbed. Cynthia made a sudden, impulsive, sympathetic movement toward her, then drew back and resumed her knitting. After a moment Barbara's crying eased; she raised her face and sniffed a few times. Cynthia handed her a tissue from Toby's box on the cocktail table.

"Blow," Cynthia said.

Obediently Barbara blew her nose a few times, then wiped her wet eyes with the heel of her hand.

"Oh Cynthia, why can't everything be— be *nice*?"

"I know just what you mean, dear." Cynthia nodded, busily knitting. "Sometimes it's very difficult to understand why the world doesn't devote itself to making us happy. But that's not the way things work. And we must understand it and get on with the business of living."

"Well, even supposing I did—love David, I mean—what difference would that make?"

"What difference?" Cynthia cried, as aghast as she was capable of being. "Good gracious! All the difference in the world!"

"But David doesn't love me," Barbara mourned.

"What difference does that make?"

"What difference?" Barbara cried. "All the difference in the world! Why should I love him, and he not me? I might marry him if he loved me like Toby loves you."

"Oh child," Cynthia said, smiling sweetly. "Toby doesn't love me."

"What?" Barbara whispered, horrified. "Cynthia, what are you saying? Toby not love you? That's nonsense. He'd be lost without you. He may not love you as much as you love him, but he does love you."

"Oh no," Cynthia said serenely. "Toby has a very great affection for me; I know that. But he doesn't love me. He just loves the idea of my worshiping him."

"And you've settled for that?"

(It was a good day for aghastness in the Marlow manse.)

"I've settled for that," Cynthia agreed.

"All your life?"

"All my life. It *has* been my life—my love for Toby. That's all I've ever asked, that he allow me to love him."

"Well, that's not enough for me," Barbara said definitely.

"Mmm," Cynthia said, peering down at her work and counting stitches. "It's your decision, dear."

There was silence a long moment while Barbara considered what she had just heard. Then . . .

"I think I'd like a glass of wine," she said. "Would you like something?"

"That would be nice. A little Scotch for me, dear."

Barbara rose from the floor with some difficulty. First she rolled onto one hip, then bent her legs, then used the couch to lean on, then straightened her legs slowly, hauling herself erect. Cynthia watched these panting efforts closely, but made no effort to help. Barbara, finally standing, bent slightly backward, duck-footed to the liquor cart, and began pouring drinks.

That was when an invisible observer would become absolutely certain that Toby was awake and listening to the conversation. For as Barbara was filling the glasses, his hand rose from the coverlet and reached piteously in her direction. But she didn't notice him; she took her own and Cynthia's glass back to the couch. Toby's hand and arm fell back sadly, forlornly.

"Oh my," Cynthia said after the first sip. "That *is* good. I'm sure it will help me count stitches. Toby taught me how to appreciate good liquor, you know. He taught me so many things."

"What kind of things?" Barbara asked, easing herself down backward onto the couch.

"Oh... how to play billiards and gamble at chemin de fer and how to faint—how to *pretend* to faint—and fall to the floor without bruising yourself, and how to use makeup, and what to do if someone insults you."

"What do you do if someone insults you?" Barbara asked, fascinated.

"Spit in his eye," Cynthia said sweetly.

"Oh well..." Barbara laughed. "That's Toby. But David isn't the man Toby is."

"He might be, dear—some day."

"Oh... maybe. But I doubt it. Toby is so open, so outgoing. He says exactly what he feels. He's not afraid to expose himself."

Cynthia dropped her needlework. Her head went back in great guffaws of laughter. She found it difficult to stop. Even Toby's chest could be seen heaving silently under the coverlet.

"Expose himself?" Cynthia gasped. "Expose himself? Well, he has done that on *very* rare occasions. But I really do think you mean Toby is willing to *reveal* his feelings."

"Oh," Barbara said. "Of course. Toby's not afraid to reveal himself."

"He enjoys it," Cynthia said. "The skunk!"

"But David isn't like that at all. He's so withdrawn, so involved in himself. He's such an egotist."

"You think Toby isn't?"

"But in a different way," Barbara argued. "Toby plays at it. It's a part he's acting. But with David, the egotism is real. 'What's my motivation?' That's all he's interested in. He's so wound up in himself, so tight. Even in bed—he's very good in bed, Cynthia—he—"

"That's nice, dear."

"But even in bed he never forgets himself, never really lets himself go. He's removed from me, apart from me. Cynthia, he's just not *passionate*. He's saying to himself, 'Now I must be passionate. Now I must be tender. Now I must be brutal.' He's playing a part, but he doesn't realize it. Toby isn't just playing like that, is he?"

"If he is"—Cynthia smiled—"he's awfully good at it."

On the couch, under the throw quilt, eyes closed, Toby Marlow nodded approvingly.

"Cynthia, I want something too," Barbara said earnestly. "It's not enough for me to sit in the audience and worship David. I want to be loved in return. I'm ready for it. Really I am. I can respond; honest I can. But just loving and not being loved in return isn't enough. Maybe you can do it, but I can't."

"It's better than nothing, dear," Cynthia said placidly.

"Oh God, is it? I don't think so. I couldn't take it for a lifetime, the way you have."

Cynthia sighed deeply and put aside her needles and yarn. She took off her glasses to stare long and thoughtfully at Barbara Evings.

"Take what?" she asked softly. "Do you think I've been punished, that I've been suffering for a lifetime? I don't want you to think as I do, you very foolish young girl, but I assure you I have no feeling of suffering or punishment. I am grateful to Toby for having given me so much happiness, and I know he feels the same way toward me. He may not love me—at least, not the way I love him—but I know, I *know* I am very dear to him. Yes. There is a tenderness. I remember I went on a tour with him once. We were in—where was it? Chicago, I think. Or perhaps Santa Fe. Some place like that. Toby had the lead in *Man and Superman*, and it was a very great success. Marvelous reviews. Worshiping audiences. Then I got sick. In Chicago or Santa Fe. Toby let the company go on without him. They flew in a replacement from New York. But Toby stayed with me and nursed me. His replacement was very, very good, and Toby didn't rejoin the company. But I never heard a word of complaint from him. Never! I knew that it hurt him to give up the tour, but he knew what he had to do. Through affection for me. Just affection. But it was enough. He nursed me until I was well. I think it was hepatitis, or perhaps it was hemorrhoids; goodness, I've had so *many* things. And then, when I was well enough to travel, we came back to New York, and he was out of work for more than a year. But he never reproached me, never regretted what he had done, never mentioned it again. So you see, dear, loving with no hope of love in return can have its rewards, unexpected rewards."

Barbara was depressed; eyes lowered, head bowed, shoulders slumped.

"I don't think David would ever nurse me," she said mournfully. "He'd just go on with the tour and leave me there."

"David is a very young man, dear."

"I don't mind that. But what scares me, why I don't want to marry him, is that I'm afraid he'll never grow up."

Cynthia put her spectacles back on, began to gather up her knitting and stuff it into a paper shopping bag from Zabar's Delicatessen.

"Well, you must make up your mind, Barbara. I try never to advise people. When your advice is bad, and they take it, they never forgive you. And when your advice is good, and they take it, they never forgive you. Oh my! That was witty, wasn't it?"

"Yes." Barbara laughed. "It was."

"Well, dear," Cynthia said, finishing her drink, "you do what you want to do. You know this is your home as long as you want it to be. Just remember that Toby and David are players, in spite of what David thinks. And players need special understanding."

"Special?"

"Oh yes." Cynthia nodded. "For instance, Toby and I never had sex when he was in rehearsal. But then after opening night, everything was all right again. Better, if the show was a hit."

"That's odd."

"Isn't it? Have you and David had sex since he's been in rehearsal?"

"No."

"Well, there you are!" Cynthia said triumphantly. "And it bothered you, didn't it?"

"Yes, it did."

"I know. You thought that just because you were pregnant, he didn't want anything to do with you."

"Yes, that's what I thought."

Cynthia leaned forward, a soft smile lighting her face, recalling another time, another place....

"I remember I thought the same thing. Toby was doing Iago when I was carrying David, and I thought he didn't like me any more because he wouldn't come near me. I thought he hated me because I was pregnant and had trapped him. But it wasn't that at all. It was because he was in rehearsal."

"I don't understand that," Barbara said, shaking her head.

"I'm sure I don't either, my dear. I'm just passing along a very odd fact: if you're married to or sleeping with an actor, you must be prepared for an absolute *dry* spell if he's in rehearsal."

"Oh Cynthia, you know so much."

"I know very little, darling. But whatever perception I do have, Toby has given me. Will you think about that?"

"Oh yes . . . yes. . . ."

"Now let's go in the kitchen and help Blanche. I think she's making lamb stew. It's Toby's favorite, you know."

The two women left the room. The moment the door closed behind them, Toby Marlow threw the coverlet aside, stumbled to his feet, staggered to the liquor cart. He poured himself a heavy whiskey with a shaking hand, took a deep gulp gratefully.

"JAYSUS H. KEE-RIST!"

He took another swallow, smaller, then drained the glass.

"Mommy," he said aloud, "can I lick the spoon?"

Then he poured another drink, added ice and a little water, and carried the glass as he stalked about the room somewhat weakly, unsteadily. He picked up the cane hanging from the wheelchair, took a few hesitant steps with it, leaning on it. Then he threw it from him angrily and paced unaided.

"'She's making lamb stew,'" he mimicked. "'It's Toby's favorite, you know.' Oh God, oh God, how long must Thou forsake me? Lamb stew, for Chrissake, and she who just said, 'Whatever perception I do have, Toby has given me.' Well, I failed miserably on the subject of lamb stew, luv!"

He laughed, freshened his drink, sat on the edge of the couch. He sipped with one hand, caressed his shiny pate with the other. The room was darkening now, but he made no effort to turn on more lights. The shadows were lengthening. Occasionally he heard muted kitchen sounds and faraway laughter. But Toby was alone, and savoring it. Finally he placed his whiskey

glass on the cocktail table and reached for the guitar
leaning against the liquor cart. He spread his knees,
placed the guitar flat across them. He made a few
experimental thrums, paused to tighten a few strings.
Then he strummed chords as he sang in a strong,
resonant, and not unmusical voice:

"'He that has and a tiny little wit,

"'With a hey, ho, the wind and the rain,

"'Must make content with his fortunes fit,

"'Though the rain it raineth every day...'"

He stopped singing but continued to flick the guitar
softly, making a rhythm by thudding the box softly
with the heel of his hand. Finally he put it aside, stood,
and began to wander again. He moved about the room,
picking up photos and theatrical memorabilia to
inspect them and then put them away gently,
remembering and smiling. Then, hands in the pockets
of his robe, head lowered, he prowled the room at a
faster pace. He stopped once to pick up his glass of
whiskey and sip. His speed increased, arms and hands
swinging free in wide gestures. He began muttering—
nothing intelligible. But as he paced, pausing frequently to sip from his glass, then resuming his prowl,
gesturing, his voice became gradually louder with
words, disjointed phrases. Finally he nodded....

"Got it!" he said, with satisfaction.

He adjusted the gooseneck lamp under which
Cynthia had been knitting. The beam of light was now
cast upward. Toby took his position in the glare; the
effect was of a spotlight. He began to declaim his "big
soliloquy," an impromptu speech the scamp had just
composed. It was roguish enough to entrance and
serious enough to make any listener believe he was
speaking the truth. He delivered this rip-off of the big
soliloquy from *Hamlet* in the grand manner. It was
heroic playing, with broad gestures, obvious expressions, coarse body movements, etc.—just the way he

wanted David to deliver the real thing. Now the words were nothing, but he overcame them by his craft. He relished the put-on—knowing the speech was not worth the effort, but his expertise making it convincing. . . .

"To love, or to be loved: that is the question.
"Whether 'tis nobler in the heart to suffer
"The slings and arrows of unrequited lust
"Or to accept with grace and dignity
"Another's sweet devotion and, by accepting,
"Give it life. To love, to hope, and by that hope
"To charge with meaning this life's hopeless days.
"To love, to hope—to dream. Ay, there's the rub!
"For in that dream of lovers what . . ."

His voice faltered, then faded, then stopped. It was silent then; even sounds from the kitchen were stilled. Toby Marlow stared at the lamp/spotlight, far away and remembering. . . .

The illumination that suddenly brightened the room was daylight, flooding through three tall windows skimpily covered with torn gauze curtains. It was a hotel room in "Chicago or Santa Fe—some place like that." It was a hotel in the grimy downtown section, close to the theatres, and if it once knew glory, you'd never know it. It had that dented, dusty, worn, splintered, sheepish look of hotel rooms that offer mattresses shared by ten thousand strangers.

The furniture was stained veneer, the wallpaper stained roses, the small rugs merely stains with fringe. There was an entrance from the hotel corridor at right. The door at left led to the bathroom. There were two beds, two chests of drawers, two chairs, two tables, two luggage racks, two lamps, two coat trees, and one awful smell.

Open valises were on the luggage racks. Coats, jackets, trousers, dresses, underwear, shoes were scattered about. There was the expected bottle of whiskey on one of the tables, with two sticky glasses. There were the remains of a breakfast on the other table: clotted coffee cups, an ashtray with a cold cigar butt, crusted dishes, half-eaten rolls, a single apple with one bite experimentally removed, then laid carefully alongside the mother.

Cynthia was in one of the beds, a sheet and thin blanket pulled up to her waist. She was younger, in her late 30s, but now pale, fragile, and moving with the deliberate slowness of the ill. She was reading a novel, pausing occasionally to take a sip of a dark brown liquid from a small medicine bottle. On the floor alongside her bed were more bottles of medicine, tissues, boxes of pills, comb, brush, mirror, makeup, etc.

Cynthia heard a key fumble in the lock and stopped her reading to look up. A younger Toby slammed the door behind him. He strode directly to the whiskey bottle, poured himself half a glass, and downed it. Then he yanked off his hat and scaled it into one corner of the room, peeled off his wig and hurled it into another corner.

"Damn! Damn! Damn!"

"Was he that good, dear?" Cynthia asked sympathetically.

"The son of a bitch was great."

"But he's your friend, Toby."

"So? That makes it all the worse. Who the hell wants to see his friends succeed? He's set for the rest of the tour. Goddamn it, Cyn, why the hell did you have to go and get the bug right now? My notices were marvelous."

"I told you to go on without me, Toby. I wouldn't mind. Truly I wouldn't."

"Ahh...screw it!" he said angrily. "I'm out, and Jack's in. Even my costumes fit him—the bastard!"

"Did you tell him how good he was?"

"Oh sure." Toby sighed. "I smiled sincerly and shook his hand. Then I tried to nudge him into the orchestra pit, but he wasn't having any. Damn it to hell, Cyn, I think you got sick deliberately."

"Of course I did, dear. I love this room; it's so comfy. I want to stay here for years and years."

Toby slumped disconsolately in one of the rickety chairs at the table. He began to examine the label on the whiskey bottle as if he had never seen it before. He didn't look at Cynthia when he spoke.

"No. I know what it was. You thought there was something between me and that kid with the balloon tits, and you wanted to break it up, so you pretended to get sick so I'd have to leave the company."

"Now you're being ridiculous," she said coldly. "I never even thought of that. Toby, I am ill. I really am."

"Oh sure," he scoffed.

"Besides, there isn't, is there?"

"Isn't what?"

"Anything between you and that girl?"

"There!" he shouted. "You see? That proves it. It's enough to drive a man to drink."

To prove it, he poured another heavy shot and drained it off as quickly as the first. Then he took a deep breath.

"Well," he said tragically, "there goes my career."

"Oh Toby, don't be so—so dramatic."

"So *dramatic*? My God, that's what I'm supposed to be. That's my job. What did the doctor say?"

"Another week. Then maybe I'll be well enough to travel."

"Another week?" he said gloomily. "Might as well be another year."

"He said my—"

"Stop right there!" Toby cried, holding up a hand. "Women's plumbing is a mystery to me, and I want it to remain a mystery."

"Toby, I'm *suffering*!"

"Well, what the hell do you think I'm doing flipping my wick? The first good job I've had in three years, and you ruin it."

"I'm sorry," she said faintly.

"Sorry. Fat lot of good that does."

"You needn't be so nasty about it."

"You have no idea how nasty I can be if I put my mind to it."

"I have an inkling, dear," she told him. "I have an inkling. May I have a whiskey, please? The doctor said it would be good for me."

Toby grudgingly poured her a thimbleful of whiskey, barely dampening the inside of the sticky glass. He brought it over to her.

"Oh thank you so much," she said. "I'll sip it slowly so I don't choke on it."

"Well, we've got to go easy on that stuff," Toby said, returning to the table and slouching down again. "I'm off the payroll, you know. If we're lucky, we'll just make it back to New York. But we've got to cut expenses to the bone."

Whereupon he poured himself a huge dollop from the same bottle.

"That's what I like most about you, dear," she said sweetly. "Your self-sacrifice."

"Shut up and heal your ass so we can get out of this hellhole."

They were silent then, shocked to quiet by his snarl. Toby, seated at one of the small tables, had his back half-turned to Cynthia's bed. She knew better than to expect him to make the first tentative offer at reconciliation.

"I really am sorry, Toby," she said softly. "About your losing the job."

He grunted.

"I know how much it meant to you."

He grunted.

"I think it was a sweet and loving thing for you to do, to stay and nurse me."

Then he turned to face her, shaking his head in wild disbelief.

"I must be out of my ever-loving mind. I could have hired a nurse for you, or asked a bellhop to look in occasionally, or *something*."

"But you didn't. Because you love me."

He grunted.

"You love me, don't you?"

"Sure."

"Can't you say it like you mean it?"

He stared at her, all cold hauteur, the Abominable Snowman attacked by swans. In his reply, his rich voice came to life. He pulled out all the stops—a full diapason. He delivered his lines for an audience of two thousand. It was a sincere boom that carried to the balcony, and every syllable was choked with deep, heartfelt emotion.

"Cynthia, I love you. I love you more than any woman I've ever known."

"Much better," she said approvingly.

"What do you want to eat?" he said.

"You."

"Don't be silly. I might catch what you've got. There's a Chinese place around the corner. Do you feel like some fantail shrimp?"

"After what the doctor did to me today," she said, "I feel *exactly* like some fantail shrimp."

"Not bad." He smiled.

"You're not angry with me any more?"

"Would it do me any good?"

"But you'll never let me forget it, will you?" she mourned. "I mean getting sick and making you leave the company. You'll keep reminding me of the sacrifice you made for me, won't you?"

"Of course."

"For years and years."

"As long as we both shall live." He nodded.

"And you're not joking. Because from now on, every time I catch you doing something dreadful, you'll weasel out of it by reminding me of the time I cost you your job."

"So?" he said. "That's normal, adult human behavior."

"Oh God, why must I love you so much?"

"Who can resist me?"

"I wish I could." She sighed. "But I can't. Toby, please don't stop letting me love you. I would die, just die."

"Love away, dear," he said cheerily. "Love away."

"And tell me again you had nothing to do with that girl."

"What girl?"

"The one with the pumpkins."

"I swear I had nothing to do with the girl with the pumpkins."

"Besides," Cynthia said, "her body isn't all that great. I saw her in the dressing room, and she has this great horrible appendicitis scar that looks like you could mail letters in it."

"What appendicitis scar?" he said. "I didn't see   "

His mouth clamped shut—too late; he had been trapped.

"You bastard!" Cynthia gasped.

She collapsed down into her bed, face in hands, weeping bitterly. Toby immediately rushed to her side. He sat on the bed, gathered her into his arms. He pressed her to him, her face against his chest. He stroked her hair, stroking, stroking...

"Love me, Cyn," he whispered. "Love me, love me, love me...."

But then the light from the gooseneck lamp in the

Marlow living room on Central Park West was there. It glowed, it shone, it beamed, haloing an exultant Toby Marlow as he concluded his grand soliloquy triumphantly, arms flung wide....

"To love, or to be loved: which is the better fate?
"For rarely do the two find a happy junction,
"But each must waste of talent and desire
"On a partner not his natural mate.
"But what care I for this philosophy?
"I love myself—and Cynthia loves me!"

SCENE THREE

Ten days later, again in the Marlows' living room, dimly lighted by flickering flames in the brick fireplace.... It was almost midnight. Barbara Evings was alone, moving slowly about in the dimness, almost drifting. She was softly crooning a folksong to herself: "Black is the color of my true love's hair..." or "I know who I love and I know where I'm going..." or something like that. Alone, enormously pregnant, singing to herself, she seemed particularly young and vulnerable.

Suddenly the hallway door banged open; David Marlow strode in. He slammed the door behind him, rushed directly to the liquor cart. Barbara lowered herself cautiously onto the couch and watched him pour a large glass of whiskey. He demolished almost half of it in one gargantuan swallow. He gagged on it, gasped, coughed. Then he took another small sip, quieted down, took a deep breath. He flopped on the couch, away from Barbara. He hunched over, head down, hands and drink between his spread knees.

"Bad?" she asked sympathetically.

"A disaster," he said dully. "Everything went wrong that could possibly go wrong."

"Isn't that what a dress rehearsal is for—to find out what can go wrong, what *is* wrong, and fix it?"

"Supposed to be." He nodded. "But it's too late to fix this performance."

"David, what *is* it?"

He sighed, took another sip of his drink. He straightened up, then slid down to a slumped position. His head was pressed against the back of the couch; he stared at the ceiling.

"It was me. I was a stick. I know it. No fire, no passion, no guts. The words came out like lumps. Cinders. Forgot my lines a dozen times. Stumbled twice. Knocked over a prop. Dropped my sword in the dueling scene. Oh, I was beautiful."

"Just nerves," she comforted him.

"Nerves? Why should I have nerves at a dress rehearsal? No, it was more than that. I was halfway through the 'What a piece of work is man' speech, and suddenly I realized I just didn't have it. No confidence. I should never have taken the part, never have tried out for it. Maybe I'm too young, too inexperienced. I'm just not ready for it. Maybe someday I will be. Maybe. Someday. But not now, not for tomorrow night. And everyone knew it. I could see it in their looks—those damned, happy, triumphant looks. The play will go down, but they'll salvage some pleasure from my failure. That's the way people are."

"Are they?"

"Sure," he said bitterly. "If they could think of any reason to cancel, it would be off the boards right now. Well . . . maybe I'll be lucky and lose my voice before tomorrow night, or step in front of a gypsy cab—or *something*."

He sighed again, finished his drink. He rose, started for the liquor cart. Then he stopped, stared around, became aware for the first time of the quietness and emptiness of the room.

"Where is everyone?" he asked Barbara.

"Gone to bed. Toby is very bad. He threw up right after dinner."

"Lamb stew?"

"No, just the soft things he's been eating lately—the cottage cheese and custard. But he couldn't keep it down. Cynthia was frightened and called Doctor Jake. He came over, and finally they got Toby to sleep. He was in awful pain."

"Moaning and groaning, I suppose?"

"Oh yes," Barbara said. "He wouldn't let a chance like that go by. He insisted on kissing us all good-by, and he left a message for you."

"Oh God, did he? The old ham! All right, what was the message?"

"He said to tell you to stop masturbating."

"Stop masturbating? What the hell's with him? I don't masturbate. Haven't since I got out of the Coast Guard. Was he delirious?"

"With Toby, it's hard to tell."

"It sure as hell is," he agreed. "Want a drink?"

"A little glass of port, please."

David replenished his own glass, poured Barbara a small glass of wine. He brought it to her, and sat closer to her this time.

"Mother with him now?" he asked.

"Yes. She and Blanche and I are going to take turns sitting up all night with him. I go on in an hour, but I couldn't sleep so I decided to wait up for you."

David was shocked.

"Sitting up with him all night? The three of you? Jesus Christ, that doesn't sound good."

"No, it isn't," she said sadly. "He's going, David. Doctor Jake told Cynthia it could be any time, and not more than a week."

"Oh God," David groaned. "That means he won't be able to see me open tomorrow night."

"No."

"Well, maybe that's for the best. That would kill him if anything would. But shouldn't he be in the hospital?"

"He won't go."

"The hell with what he wants! We'll make him go."

"Make Toby do something he doesn't want to do?"

"Jake can give him a shot, knock him out, and we'll get him over there before he knows what's happening."

"David, would you do that to Toby?"

"If it'll save his life."

"It won't. Doctor Jake says they couldn't do anything for him. He says let the man die in peace in his own home if that's what he wants."

"Die in peace?" David repeated incredulously. "That's a laugh. Toby never did anything in peace in his whole life, and he's not about to start now. He'll go kicking and screaming, in the greatest display of histrionics you've ever seen. Oh God, what an ugly, depressing, fucked-up, senseless world this is."

"Didn't Will say that better?" she mocked him.

"You mean, 'O God! O God! how weary, stale, flat, and unprofitable seem to me all the uses of this world'? Act One, Scene Two. See, I do know my lines. Yes, Will said everything better. And he deserves a better actor than me."

They were silent a long moment. Then she moved

clumsily along the couch, sliding closer to him. She put a hand on his arm.

"Are you hungry, David? I can make you a sandwich. There's some cold roast beef."

"No, thanks. My stomach's a knot. I couldn't swallow. I'm all wound up."

"Do you want me to sleep with you tonight?" she asked softly. "I will, if you want me to."

He touched her face tenderly.

"No, luv. I want you, but not out of pity."

"We can't *do* anything," she said. "Well . . . maybe I could do something. Or we could just lie there. I don't think you should be alone tonight."

"I appreciate it," he said, somewhat formally, "but no, thanks. I'll be all right. I'll get through this by myself."

"You won't give and you won't take," she said angrily.

He pulled away from her and stared. . . .

"What the hell is that supposed to mean? Come on—let's have it. It won't make this night any worse than it's been. Nothing can do that."

"Oh . . . what's the use, David?" she said wearily. "We've been through all this before. Let's just try to stay friends. Can't we do that?"

"Jesus Christ, you're a walking soap opera! 'No, David, I will not marry you. But can't we still be friends! I'll cherish the memory of you forever.' What shit!"

"Toby would have played those lines better," she said.

He rose in a fury and began stalking about the room, his voice growing louder. . . .

"Toby, Toby, Toby!" he cried. "That's all I've been hearing all my life. 'Toby can do it better. You'll never be the player Toby is. Go ask Toby how to do it.' Goddamn it, I'm grown up and I'm my own man. I don't care how Toby would deliver those lines or how Toby would play that scene. I'm me—*David* Marlow! I'll never be Toby, and thank God for that! Don't any of you realize what a ridiculous clown he is? With his posturings and grand manner and heroic acting and gestures and a style that were hilarious thirty years ago? The man's a silly old fossil! Can't you see that? He's living in a never-never land of Duse and Barrymore and W.C. Fields. Gone, all gone. You can't act that way any more. You'd be laughed off the stage. People want to think, to know.... You've got to go deeper, down, down, within yourself, to reveal the truth."

"What truth?" she asked quietly.

"What?" he cried, still excited. "What?"

"What truth must you reveal, David?"

"Well ... the truth, just the truth. Is there more than one truth?"

"Isn't there? For Hamlet and for Othello? For Duke Mantee and for Billy Budd. For Stanley Kowalski and for King Arthur? They're all truths, aren't they? Different, but true."

"I won't play at them," he shouted stubbornly. "I won't pretend."

"You can," she said. "I know you can."

"I can't."

"Remember that Sunday morning the baby was born?"

He looked at her, flummoxed.

"Born?"

"Well ... conceived."

"How can you know?" he scoffed.

"I *do*! I do know. *That* morning you pretended. And it was beautiful. Beautiful...."

They gazed at each other, remembering, and suddenly the Marlows' living room was wiped out by a sudden torrent of white light as if a master electrician had thrown the switch of floods, spots, foots, borders. It was a milky glare blazing Barbara Evings' former loft apartment. A single long room dwindling to a blur. The furnishings were minimal, all painted white. Even the few framed graphics on the walls seemed to be hidden behind white silk gauze, or perhaps the viewer's eyeballs had been lightly smeared with Vaseline.

It was a lazy Sunday morning in this out-of-focus scene. Barbara and David were seated at a small white bistro table, on white wire ice-cream parlor chairs. Both were barefoot, wearing white terry-cloth robes. On the table was a white pitcher of coffee and a white china platter of croissants. Farther back in the hazy room, drenched with light, was a folding bed—really a wire cot with a thin mattress; the type of bed that can be doubled up and wheeled into a closet.

The entire room had a pleasing simplicity, a peaceful emptiness, a kind of vacant charm. And over all hung the quiet languor of Sunday morning.

David selected a croissant from the platter and held it up near his mouth and ear, like a French telephone.

"Hello?" he said. "Tom?"

Barbara looked at him a moment, puzzled. Then her face cleared, she selected a croissant daintily, and held it to her ear and mouth.

"I'm sorry," she said. "I think you have the wrong number."

"Isn't this 555-1212?"

"No, it's 4X7-G9T3-19678326-K."

"I beg your pardon. I must have dialed the wrong number."

"That's all right," Barbara said. "Could have happened to anyone. It's nice to hear a wrong number apologize."

"Yes. Well, good-by now."

"Good-by," she said.

They paused, looked speculatively at each other. After a moment Barbara ate a bit of her croissant, crunching off the tip. David did the same with his croissant, then moved it closer to his mouth to speak.

"Hello?" Barbara said eagerly.

"Look," David said. "I called last night. I asked for a man named Tom. Or perhaps Bernie. You answered. I had dialed the wrong number, and I apologized."

"I remember," Barbara said. "And . . . ?"

"Well . . . I'm not an obscene phone caller or anything like that. Except . . ."

"Except what?"

"I like your voice," he said with a rush. "Look, if I'm annoying you or offending you, please tell me and I'll hang up, and I swear I'll never call you again."

"Why are you calling me now?"

"Well . . . as I said, I like your voice. And . . ."

"And?"

"And I just wanted to say hello."

"Oh," she said. "Well . . . hello."

"You won't be offended if I call again?" he asked.

"No. I won't be offended."

During this exchange, each nibbled on his croissant while the other spoke. Now, pastries reduced to crumbs, each selected a new croissant from the platter, took a sip of coffee, and the dialogue continued as before. Both were deliberately solemn, deadpan, but as the exchange progressed, a certain tension began to build; the "play acting" began to cut close to the bone, and what began as fantasy and sleepy Sunday-morning nuttiness started to take on a significance neither had anticipated. David raised his croissant. . . .

"Good evening!" he said cheerfully.

"Hello!" she caroled into her croissant.

"How are you?"

"I've got a little cold. Can't you hear?"

"What are you taking for it?"

"What are you offering?"

"Ho ho. Look, I said it last night: if you don't want me to call, if I'm bothering you, for God's sake tell me. I'm not a fiend, really I'm not."

"If you are, you're a very *nice* fiend."

"Then I can call you again?"

"If you like..."

Their fantasy had begun lazily, drawled. But now the tempo began to pick up; they spoke faster and, curiously, they no longer looked at each other, but peered intently at their coffee cups or croissant phones. Nibbling, of course.

"Hello?" Barbara said.

"Hi," David said. "It's me again. How's the cold?"

"Better, thank you. I was afraid it might be the flu or a virus. But now I think it's just the sniffles. May I ask you a personal question?"

"Must I answer?"

"No. Of course not."

"Sure, go ahead—ask."

"What's your name?"

David paused a moment.

"Romeo," he said finally.

"That's a nice name," she said. "Polish?"

"Swedish, ekshully. What's yours?"

"Juliet."

"Oh? French?"

"Assyrian, ekshully. On my mother's side. The left one. My father is an Irish setter."

"My father is a paranoid," David said.

"Lovely country that."

"Oh yes," he agreed. "Especially in the spring."

"How old are you, Romeo?" she asked.

"I'm fifteen."

"And what do you want to be when you grow up?"

"Sixteen. How old are you?"

"Thirteen," she said, "going on twelve."

"Strange," he said. "I had pictured you as a much younger woman. Do you work?"

"What else?"

"What do you do?"

"I'm an opera singer. Contralto. But I moonlight as a stewardess on a ferry boat."

"They have their own boats now?"

"What do you do?"

"I'm a brain surgeon," he said. "But I moonlight as a short-order cook. My limit is two eggs. Got anyone? A man, I mean?"

"A few," she said. "Nothing serious. Do you have a woman?"

"Yes. I've been seeing her for years. Since I was six."

"Going to marry her?"

"I suppose so," he said. "Eventually. Life isn't all bubble gum, is it?"

"No," she said, picking up on his sudden seriousness. "It isn't."

"You sound down tonight."

"I am...down."

"I guess I shouldn't have called."

"No, no. I'm glad you did. It's hearing a human voice. You know?"

"Oh God, do I ever know!" he said. "Will you call me—some time?"

"I may."

"Please do. I want you to. If I'm not in, please try again. I have crazy hours."

"How tall are you?"

"I'm almost four feet."

"Goodness. I'll have to wear heels. Good night, Romeo."

"Are you really glad I called?"

"Yes. I'm really glad."

"That's nice. Good night, Juliet."

They both reached for new croissants. They were

becoming troubled—well, perhaps not troubled but stirred by their manic dialogue. Maybe they sensed their pretense had taken on a life of its own; they could not control how it might develop. Their make-believe had suddenly assumed a stature and dignity they had not intended. My God, it was *significant*! And who knew where or how it might end? Still, they were too involved and too curious to get off.

"Hello," Barbara said.

"Oh! *You* called *me*!"

"I surely did."

"Loverly," he gurgled. "How's the cold?"

"Much better, thank you. And I bought a new hat today, and that helped."

"What's it like?"

"The hat? Like a man's fedora. Wide, slouch brim. Makes me look like Ava Gardner in that African picture with Clark Gable."

"I look a little like Clark Gable," he said. "Around the knees. What color is the hat?"

"A deep red."

"Sounds marvelous."

"It does wonders for me. I wore it home and bookkeepers whistled at me. Great for my bedraggled ego."

"Listen..." he said hesitantly, "do you think we should see each other? You know—meet?"

"No," she said firmly. "I don't. Do you?"

"I guess not. Let's keep it like this."

"No disappointments this way."

"Right," he said stiffly. "No disappointments. How's the job?"

"Shitty. And yours?"

"Shitty. Anything doing in the romance department?"

"Very quiet. And you?"

"The usual," he said. "More of the same. No

problems, but boring, boring, boring."

"Are you angry with me?" she asked.

"Angry? Of course not. Why should I be angry?"

"I don't know. But there's something in your voice. You think we should see each other?"

"Oh no. No. You were absolutely right. Avoid disappointments. Yes, that's the right thing to do."

"Will you call me tomorrow night?"

"Sure."

"Promise?"

"Of course," he said, somewhat coldly. "I promise. I'll call tomorrow night. I'll make a note of it."

They were tense now, gobbling up their croissants. It teetered, the scene, and they sensed it could go either way. One wrong word, a tonal quality. . . . But neither had the courage to end it. The risk was exciting. They plugged their pastries into their ears.

"Hi, Juliet," he sang.

"You didn't call me last night," she said stonily.

"I know," he said softly. "Not that I didn't want to. But I got involved in a kind of a party."

"Your woman?" she said coldly.

"Yes."

"Is she nice?"

"Of course she's nice. Unexciting but nice."

"Did you have fun?"

"Not much. What did you do?"

"I had a date," she said firmly.

"Fun?"

"Oh . . . I guess. Dinner at a new Italian restaurant. It was so-so. Then we went to one of those Greek places where everyone throws soup plates at the dancers. He saw me home to my door, and that was that. I didn't ask him in, in case you're wondering."

"Yes, I was."

"So was I," she said, "about an hour later. Then I

took a pill and went to sleep. Do you take sleeping pills?"

"Doesn't everyone?"

"Oh God, Romeo," she said, thawing, "there's got to be more to it than this. Listen..."

"What?"

"Don't stop calling me. Please."

"You!" he cried exultantly. "*You*! Don't *you* stop calling *me*! I need it."

"I know, I know," she said. "How awful."

"Isn't it."

"Romeo."

"Juliet."

They sensed they had successfully skirted some horrible chasm, some terrible fate. Now they could look directly at each other and smile, gnawing their pastries and waiting to see how the play ended. They leaned toward each other across the little bistro table, excited and anticipating. The croissants were held in trembling hands....

"Hello?" Barbara said nervously.

"Hi, Juliet."

"Romeo! I'm *so* happy you called."

"What are you doing?"

"Counting the walls. I'm so fucking bored." She paused a moment, then: "Do you mind my using words like that?"

"Words like 'bored'?"

"Smart-ass. You know what I mean. Do you mind?"

"Four-letter words?" he asked.

"That's right," she said. "Like 'love.' Do you mind?"

"Of course I don't mind. How are you?"

"I am very well, thank you. And how are you?"

"I am very well, thank you," he answered. "Well, now that we've got all the polite shit out of the way, I want to tell you about an article I read. It was about some survey they made about how bachelors live and their life expectancy and all that."

"Are you a bachelor, Romeo?"

"No, I'm married and have ten children and I'm calling from home."

"I wouldn't be a bit surprised."

"Yes, you silly dear, I'm a bachelor."

"Good on you."

"Are you married?"

"I was. I'm not now."

"What happened?" he asked.

"That was the problem," she replied. "Nothing happened. What about this article you read about bachelors?"

"Well, it said bachelors die off faster than married men. They commit suicide more often, they have a higher percentage of mental disorders, and they end up doing swell things like lifting little girls' skirts and watching apartments across the way through telescopes."

"Does that scare you—lifting my skirt?"

"Strange, but that doesn't scare me."

"Did this article say anything about women bachelors?"

"No."

"Double it in spades. Fun it ain't."

"I know. Do you ever see your ex husband?"

"Occasionally. We're still friends."

"Any children?"

"No," she said.

"That's lucky."

"Yes. Lucky. Are you really four feet tall?"

"Almost."

"What color hair?" she asked.

"Green. What color is yours?"

"Blue. And I work very hard to keep it that way.

Listen, Romeo, I have a very personal question to ask you."

"Ask away."

"Do you play Scrabble?"

"No."

"Well . . . no one's perfect."

"You are," David said. "I love you, Juliet."

"Do you?" she said wonderingly.

"I'm beginning to think so. What are you doing this weekend?"

"Going away. Up to the lake. A married couple I know."

"Will they have a man for you?"

"Of course. They always do. A man with nostrils. Do you have nostrils?"

"Naturally."

"That flutter?"

"No, my nostrils don't flutter. I'm going away, too. A dude ranch."

"With your woman?"

"Yes."

"That article about bachelors really scared you, didn't it?"

"It surely did."

"Going to propose?" she asked.

"It didn't scare me that much," he said.

"It only hurts when you laugh," she advised.

"I know. Can I call you on Monday?"

"Do you have to ask?"

"I'll tell you all about the dude ranch, and you tell me about the guy with the fluttering nostrils."

"I could tell you all about him right now, and I haven't even met him yet. A blank."

"That's what the dude ranch will be. A blank. I hate horses. They're so fucking superior."

"Why are you going?"

"She promised a mare."

"How's the sex?"

"Well..." he said. "You know. Comme ci, comme ça."

"The story of my life," she said. "Are you in bed right now?"

"Yes."

"Naked?"

"Yes," he said in a low voice. "Are you?"

"Yes. Let's breathe heavily at each other for a while."

"Don't joke about it," he said, hurt.

"I'm sorry," she said. "I shouldn't have. Please forgive me."

"Sure."

"I joke about things too much, I know. I joke because...well, you know. I *have* to joke."

"I know, Juliet."

"Do you really love me?"

"I really do."

"I love you, Romeo. Can you take that?"

"Can I ever! Say it again."

"I love you, Romeo."

Suddenly, inexplicably excited by their sappy dialogue, Barbara and David rose simultaneously to their feet and moved toward the bed, turning their backs on the croissant crumbs. They didn't rush, but they didn't dawdle either. Their white robes dropped magically away; their movements seemed to slow as they swam gracefully naked through the aquarium of light. The bed loomed hazily out of the glare, as through a white scrim, and the room and time had the elusive quality of a vaguely remembered dream.

David lay on the bed, on his back, his engorged cudgel pointing accusingly at God. Barbara stood at the bedside, then leaned forward to touch him lightly, lovingly....

"Romeo, Romeo," she murmured, "what a big little boy you are."

The white glare sheened their flesh, made faint lilac shadows in the hollows of their bodies when they moved....

"Horses are so fucking superior," he repeated in a whisper.

Obediently, with more crave than grace, she swung one leg wide across him and, with a minimum of fuss, impaled herself, sitting atop him, knees drawn up alongside his waist. Hands on his shoulders, she leaned forward so her long hair enveloped their faces. Unseen by bachelors with telescopes, they kissed and kissed....

His hands sought the long muscles of her hard back, swoop of waist, flare of ass. They pulled her to him with slowly increasing urgency. She straightened up astride him, pushed her hair back with both hands, a movement she knew would please him, and hopefully inflame....

It did! His eyes were half shut now, his mouth half open, and she began to move, fitting her gait to his. Their groans were soft and dignified, almost lost in the not unmusical squeaks and twangs of the wire cot....

Here their dialogue was improvised, consisting of equal measures of passion and gibberish. The names David, Barbara, Romeo, and Juliet were heard frequently, along with reiterated protestations of love and undying allegiance, interspersed by increasing sobs of pleasure, moans of delight, and similar stuff. Experienced players know how to do this sort of thing well.

Their litany was suddenly interrupted by a loud metallic *crack*! clearly heard but, understandably, disregarded by the players. A cold-eyed critic would have soon become aware that an important part of the bed—a rigid strut that held it in its unfolded position—had broken under the unusual strains placed upon it. Before the horrified stare of such a critic, the bed, with most of the weight and now violent shocks concentrated in the middle, began to fold up like a giant clam shell lined with mattress and sheets.

Slowly the head section and the foot section lifted their legs from the floor. The two halves wavered in the air, then paused a brief moment. But the players, now locked in the final anguish of their desire, were oblivious to their danger. If anything, their labors increased, in tempo and fury, and so intense was their concentration that their howls of bliss drowned out the cracking that resumed beneath them.

David's head, shoulders, and upper torso rose slowly, mysteriously, from his waist, as his legs did from his hips. As the bed inexorably folded up, so did he, and Barbara was forced to sit erect, her nose elevated, to escape suffocation.

But they were determined not to be halted short of their goal by accident, war, or Act of Princes. Their final scream of triumph rang out, somewhat muffled, even as the perfidious bed completed its closing with a *chwung*!, entrapping them in closer embrace than ever lovers dreamt.

The room and memories went dark, to be replaced by the dimness and flickering flames in the fireplace of the Marlows' living room. David and the pregnant Barbara were back in their original positions: she sitting on the couch, he standing nearby.

"That Sunday morning the baby was made," she said dreamily. "I know it."

"How do you know?" he asked.

"I just do."

"Well... maybe." He shrugged. "We were lucky to get out of that damned thing alive."

"I just wanted you to remember that you *can*

pretend. You did that morning. And you can again."

"That morning was—well, just between us. It has nothing to do with my job, with acting. I won't pretend at that."

"Oh no," she said. "You'll be yourself, won't you? Your own sweet self. You'll go deeper, down, down, within yourself to reveal 'the truth.' *Your* truth. And just what is that? Something I wouldn't marry in a million years. So locked up inside yourself, closed off to me, so conscious of your own thoughts and motivations that you lose all conception of what the playwright is trying to say. The writer—that poor man! At least he's *trying* to create something, to open a window, to make the world a little wider, a little bigger." (*Hear, hear!—Author.*) "But you take what he's done and squeeze it down so it reflects only *you* and has no more meaning than *you* can bring to it."

She hauled herself to her feet with difficulty, shaking off his proffered hand angrily. She waddled to the door, yanked it open. Then she turned to glare at him. . . .

"Toby was right," she yelled. "Why don't you stop masturbating, you—you *organist*!"

He looked at her in astonishment, shaking his head.

"What?" he said. "What was that? Why am I an organist?"

"An organist is a man who spills his seed upon the ground. It's from the Bible."

"Oh Jesus," he said, "you mean *onanist,* not organist."

"Well, what the hell's the difference?" she shouted, slamming out.

SCENE FOUR

TOBY MARLOW WAS DYING—and didn't care who knew it. He lay propped up on bolsters, glaring indignantly at the world, in his own bed, in the Marlows' bedroom. Cynthia, Blanche, and Barbara hovered nearby. David stood helplessly to one side. The scene was as artfully composed as a crèche. The room was brilliantly illuminated with chandelier, lamps, the red neon sign flashing "Marlow... Marlow..."

"Turn on the goddam lights!" Toby cried petulantly. "Why is it so dark in here?"

"The lights are on, dear," Cynthia said softly. "All the lights."

"Then bring some candles," Toby insisted. "For the love of God, give me some light."

Blanche went over to the commode, lighted tapers in twin candelabra. She placed one on the table next to Toby's bed. She held the other close to his face.

"Light, Toby," she said.

"Who's that? Who's that?"

"Blanche, Toby."

"Blanche, the horse. We never did fuck, did we, babe?"

"No, Toby. We never did."

"In the next world, I promise. Where's David?"

"I'm here, Father," he said, stepping forward.

"'Father.' That's the first you've called me that."

"Yes. The first time."

"Soon enough. Soon enough. Why aren't you at the theatre?"

"There's time Toby. There's time."

"No, no. You can't be late. Not professional. Makeup and costume. Do you have a dresser?"

"No, no dressers. We help each other."

"I had a dresser," Toby said. "Once. Blanche was a dresser, weren't you, Blanche?"

"Yes, I—"

"Cyn?" he cried out. "Cyn? Are you there? Where the hell is Cyn?"

"I'm here, Toby."

"Hold my hand," he said, and she took his hand and continued to hold it to the end. "Cyn. Dear Cynthia. Cyn, Cyn, Cyn. That's how you caught me. Captured me. By sin! You grabbed me by the balls, hung on, and never would let go."

"Yes, Toby. That's how I did it."

"Barbara?" he asked. "She here?"

"I'm here, Toby."

"I met you too late, sweet. Too late. What a brangle-buttock game we could have had. And rub the

bacon...'Ring down the curtain, the farce is over.'
Who wrote that, shithead?"

"I don't know, Toby," David said.

"Someone did," Toby murmured. "'Ring down the
curtain, the farce is over.' Bad line. But there are no bad
parts, just... How many sides do you have, David?"

"What? I don't understand."

"In the old days... in the old days..."

"Shhh, dear," Cynthia soothed. "Just lie quietly.
Try not to talk."

"Not talk? Why don't you tell me not to breathe?
'Give sorrow words; the grief that does not speak
whispers the o'er-fraught heart and bids it break.'
David? What?"

"Macbeth," David said.

"Yes. Will again. Oh how lovely! The dear, dear
man. I'm going to be in hell with Will. They'd never let
him into heaven, he who knew so much of vice and
lechery. 'All in all, I'd rather be in Philadelphia.' That
was W. C. Fields. I knew him, you know. His epitaph.
He called Chaplin a goddamn ballet dancer. Sides.
When we didn't have mimeograph or Xerox machines,
David, that was how you got your part. Not the entire
script, but just the pages that had your lines and cues.
So you judged the importance of the part by the
number of sides you got."

"But not always," Blanche said.

"Right," Toby said faintly. "Not always. You might
be a butler and have forty-five sides, but each typed
sheet would only have your 'Yes, milord' or 'No,
milord' and your cues on it. The trick was getting a big
number of sides in sequence, a real scene. Right,
Blanche?"

"Right."

"Right, Cynthia?"

"Right, Toby. The most number of sides I ever had
was nine."

"Once. . . ." he said, "once I had three thousand, four hundred, and eighty-nine, in one play."

"Oh Toby. . . ." Cynthia said.

"I did! I did! Four thousand, three hundred, and ninety-eight. Sides. How many sides have I had in my lifetime . . . how many sides . . . ?"

"Do you want to sleep now, dear?" she said gently.

"No, I do not—*Oh, Jesus*!"

He groaned in agony, jerked halfway up, hugging his midsection.

"Squeeze my hand," Cynthia said. "Is the pain bad?"

"Screw the pain," he gasped, falling back. "I was hissed off the stage at the Palladium. Is there any pain worse than that? Cynthia. . . ."

"I'm here, Toby."

"We're married now, aren't we, Cyn?"

"Yes, Toby, we're married."

"And my bastard shithead is now my own dear, sweet shithead. Is he at the theatre?"

"No, Father. I'm here. There's time, there's time."

"No. No time, no time. Barbara? Are you there? I can't see you."

"Here, Toby."

"Kiss me, luv," he murmured. "On the lips." She leaned over and kissed him on the lips. "Oh," he breathed. "Oh, Cyn, I may go away for a little while. With Barbara."

"But you'll come back to me," she said.

"Oh yes. Oh yes. I always come back . . . to you. . . .'

There was no more talk, for a while. The door opened slowly, and Jacob Ostretter and Julius Ostretter, both clad in black, entered quietly with their identical wives, in their gold lamé dresses and high, teased beehive hairdoos. The four took up stations at the corners of Toby's bed, standing erect with hands folded in front, shockingly similar to the honor guard at the bier of an important personage.

"Who's there?" Toby cried. "Who's there?"

"Friends, Toby," Jacob Ostretter said.

"Friends," he repeated. "Friends and lovers. Oh, what a life that was! 'Think only this when I have gone: that there was laughter, love, and tears as sweet as wine.' Who wrote that, David?"

"I don't know, Father."

"I wrote that. *I*. Toby Marlow. A player. I wrote that. Yes...I did...just now..."

The lights were gradually dimming now, from the rear of the room forward, all growing darker, darker...

"Get thee to a theatre, go!" Toby shouted.

"There is time," David repeated.

"No time. No time. Shuck off your husk, my legal and passionless son. Throw off that shell that— Cynthia, what is that fish that has a shell?"

"Shrimp?"

"No. Blanche?"

"Lobster?"

"No. Barbara?"

"A kind of crustacean?"

"Crustacean! Beautiful word. Why must you be a crustacean, blood of my blood and seed of my seed? Open yourself and throw off your crust, you sweet, sweet shithead. Give. Please give. You have it; I know you have it. Are you not my legal and devoted heir? I am in you, and all you must learn is to give and spend. Give all and spend all, and never fear the well runs dry because...because...Cynthia, what do I want to say?"

"You've said it, Toby."

"Have I? Have I said it all? Thank God for that. It was a good run, a good run. And they applauded. Most of the time. I wouldn't change.... Remember, in...in some place...She came to my dressing room with a single rose. Was that you, Cyn?"

"Yes, Toby. I did that."

"You were a lousy player, Cyn."

"I know Toby."

"But a marvelous fuck. You were always a marvelous fuck, Cynthia."

"Thank you, Toby," she said, quite sincerely.

"Is that your hand?" he asked.

"Yes, it's my hand."

"Good. Good. You know when Barrymore—that was John. Yes, John. Not Lionel or Ethel. Well, someone said to John, 'Did Hamlet really seduce Ophelia?' And John said, 'Well...maybe in the Chicago company.' No, no. That's not the story. Oh...Now...When John Barrymore was going down, defeated by the demon rum and his own terror, he saw a very young and pretty girl—Barbara, are you listening?"

"I'm listening, Toby."

"It was a good run, a good run. He said—John Barrymore said—'So much to do, so little time.' Yes. I could have...I might have...Ahh, the hell with it. It's getting late."

"Hang on, you son of a bitch," Blanche said, weeping.

"O!" he said. "I can't! I can't any more. Hoc in spiritum sed non in corpore. That's Latin. I know a little bit of Latin. I know a little bit of everything. Cynthia?"

"I'm here, Toby."

"I loved you all the time." he said. "All the time."

"I knew that, Toby," she said, not weeping. "I knew it."

"Good. Good. David, open yourself to..."

The lights had gradually dimmed until there was now just a circle of soft radiance about the bed. There was no more talk. Toby Marlow, player, had died.

Barbara dropped heavily to her knees and took his other hand to kiss it. The Ostretters were immobile. Blanche was weeping silently, making no effort to cover her face. Cynthia, still clutching Toby's dead hand, did not move.

"'Now cracks a noble heart,'" David said. "'Good-night...'"

But he could not finish Horatio's speech. He began sobbing and fell to his knees at his father's bedside, embracing the dead man. As he wept uncontrollably, footlights came on, a spotlight glared, and when the still weeping David stood and faced the audience, he was the only one seen clearly; the others, in postures of grief, were in semidarkness. David strode to the footlights, challenging the audience. He flung his arms wide and began the big solioquy from *Hamlet*, with grand gestures, in the heroic manner, opening himself to the world....

"'To be, or not to be: that is the question.

"'Whether 'tis nobler in the mind to suffer the...'"

He continued declaiming, *playing* the role, as...

...the curtain falls.

Bestsellers from Berkley
The books you've been hearing about—and want to read

__**THE BIDDERS** 04606-4—$2.75
John Baxter

__**TROIKA** 04662-1—$2.75
David Gurr

__**ZEBRA** 04635-4—$2.95
Clark Howard

__**THE FIRST DEADLY SIN** 04692-3—$2.95
Lawrence Sanders

__ **THE THIRD WORLD WAR:**
AUGUST 1985 05019-X—$3.50
General Sir John Hackett, et al.

__**THE PIERCING** 04563-3—$2.50
John Coyne

__ **THE WINNER'S CIRCLE** 04500-5—$2.50
Charles Paul Conn

__ **MOMMIE DEAREST** 04444-0—$2.75
Christina Crawford

__ **NURSE** 04685-0—$2.75
Peggy Anderson

__ **THE SIXTH COMMANDMENT** 04271-5—$2.75
Lawrence Sanders

__**THE FOUR HUNDRED** 04665-6—$2.75
Stephen Sheppard

__**THE HEALERS** 04451-3—$2.75
Gerald Green

Available at your local bookstore or return this form to:

Berkley Book Mailing Service
P.O. Box 690
Rockville Centre, NY 11570

Please send me the above titles. I am enclosing $_____
(Please add 75¢ per copy to cover postage and handling). Send check or money order—no cash or C.O.D.'s. Allow six weeks for delivery.

NAME_____

ADDRESS_____

CITY_____STATE/ZIP_____ 1D

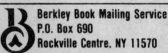